"Are You Sorry You Invited Me to Spend the Week with You, Alex?"

"No, I'm not sorry," he returned. "But I had expected you to say no."

"I almost did say no." Her words were barely audible over the crackling blaze in the fireplace.

"Which brings us back to the reason you agreed. Especially in view of the fact that I've made my intentions pretty plain."

Involuntarily, she reached out to him, and that one small movement was all that was necessary. He pulled her to him. The sudden contact with his hard chest sent shock waves through her. He held her like that for a long time, stroking the fine golden hair that flowed down her bare back. She could feel his heart thudding noisily in his chest—or was it her own?

PAMELA LIND

loves to work with words and has always wanted to be a writer. Her hobbies include sewing, tennis, horseback riding and, of course, writing.

Dear Reader:

SILHOUETTE DESIRE is an exciting new line of contemporary romances from Silhouette Books. During the past year, many Silhouette readers have written in telling us what other types of stories they'd like to read from Silhouette, and we've kept these comments and suggestions in mind in developing SILHOUETTE DESIRE.

DESIREs feature all of the elements you like to see in a romance, plus a more sensual, provocative story. So if you want to experience all the excitement, passion and joy of falling in love, then SILHOUETTE DESIRE is for you.

I hope you enjoy this book and all the wonderful stories to come from SILHOUETTE DESIRE. I'd appreciate any thoughts you'd like to share with us on new SILHOUETTE DESIRE, and I invite you to write to us at the address below:

Karen Solem
Editor-in-Chief
Silhouette Books
P.O. Box 769
New York, N.Y. 10019

PAMELA LIND
Past Forgetting

Silhouette Desire
Published by Silhouette Books New York
America's Publisher of Contemporary Romance

SILHOUETTE BOOKS, a Simon & Schuster Division of
GULF & WESTERN CORPORATION
1230 Avenue of the Americas, New York, N.Y. 10020

ISBN: 0-671-45514-1

First Silhouette Books printing November, 1982

10 9 8 7 6 5 4 3 2 1

America's Publisher of Contemporary Romance

Printed in the U.S.A.

1

He stood impassively amidst the din, allowing it to wash over him in great babbling waves. Perhaps it was his unique vantage point that allowed him to remain aloof. Or possibly it was simply the nature of the man. He didn't really think about the reason, since he was not given to introspection. All he knew was that he didn't want to be here.

His gray eyes focused briefly on the stunning redhead across the crowded room. She seemed to sense his attention immediately and turned to him with a sensual smile. She quickly disengaged herself from a group and came toward him, voluptuous curves straining against the clinging fabric of the gown.

"Let's go." The phrase was clipped, indicating quite clearly that he expected her to obey.

"But, Alex, darling, we just got here. You promised you would stay for an hour." Her voice was husky, and her expertly made-up green eyes beseeched him. Her lacquered nails crept up the broad expanse of his dinner jacket. She loved to tease.

"The hour's up." His tone was the same as before, and she recognized his growing irritation. Nonetheless, she was about to protest once more, when there was a loud tapping of metal against glass. They both turned as the room suddenly became silent and expectant.

"Ladies and gentleman, your attention please." The speaker ceased tapping a metal stirrer against the large cocktail shaker and smiled indulgently at them. He was a small, nondescript, middle-aged man. If he had not been one of Hollywood's most honored producer-directors, he might have been a tailor or perhaps a shoe salesman.

Jack Destler paused for effect. There were quiet murmurings from the assembled group. They had all been waiting for this.

"I promised you a surprise, and you are about to get one." The smile returned briefly as he noted the air of hushed expectation that hovered in the room.

"As you all know, I have just completed a film." All Hollywood knew that. Jack loved nothing more than to stir up curiosity—and then leave it unsatisfied.

So, Hollywood knew only that this film was, in Jack's characteristically modest words, "the definitive film on the sixties." They knew that the title was "The Winds of Change," and that the male lead was one of Hollywood's rising young stars. Most of the curiosity, however, was centered around the female lead. She had been made tantalizingly unavailable to them—

either through her own choice, or at Jack's insistence. Or perhaps a combination of the two.

"Tonight, I will give you a preview of that film." The murmurs grew louder. "We have finished editing about half the film, and you are about to see the results." He gave up the attempt to say anything more as the noise overwhelmed him.

Most of the guests knew the way to his private screening room and hurried off in that direction without waiting for any further invitation.

"Come on. We're leaving." Alex grasped her hand and began to walk away.

But she balked, pulling against him. "Alex, I want to see this. I've heard it's the best thing he's ever done."

As soon as she had his attention, she pressed her point.

"Besides, how would it look if we left now? Jack would be insulted, and he's too important to insult."

He raised an inquiring brow. "Important to whom?"

"To me, of course. Please, darling. We'll leave right after the screening." She gave him her most seductive smile. "I'll make it up to you, I promise."

The gray eyes swept over her, considering. "All right."

They followed the others and entered the already darkened room just as the screen came to life.

It began abruptly—without the usual credits. Television film footage provided a rapid-fire chronology of the more memorable events of the sixties: the assassinations of John Kennedy, Robert Kennedy and Martin Luther King; the Watts riots and Mayor John Lindsay walking the streets of Harlem; the antiwar protests; the horrors of Vietnam; Kent State; and Haight-Ashbury. Over the high-quality sound system came the slightly husky but pure voice of a woman singing a folk song whose poignant lyrics contrasted with the horrors on screen.

Alex's attention wandered quickly from the screen to the voice. It had a haunting quality that intrigued him. He felt bereft when it ceased, trailing off as the last of the TV footage vanished from the screen.

And then the scene shifted abruptly to a high school graduation complete with speaker intoning the usual meaningless phrases. The camera panned over the group of graduates, not pausing until it reached the dais where the honor graduates sat in the glaring sun.

Beginning to grow restless once more, Alex shifted trying to accommodate his huge frame to the confines of the chair. His attention was wandering again.

But abruptly his eyes became riveted to the woman on screen. Even in the shapeless blue gown, her beauty was astonishing. Long silken hair of pale gold flowed from under the ridiculous mortarboard, framing a face of such perfection that at first it seemed unreal. Alex was certainly no stranger to beauty. He pursued it avidly. And he was well aware of the tricks of makeup people and cameramen, but beauty like this owed nothing to those craftsmen.

The camera closed in. Even at close range the all-seeing camera exposed no imperfections—large, startlingly blue eyes, a delicate nose and sensuously full lips. He was peripherally aware, too, of a quiet dignity and poise—and an untouched quality.

Alex was mesmerized, totally unaware of the murmurs of those around him. For the remainder of the screening, he was completely oblivious to anying else—even his own earlier discomfort. When the actress was not on the screen, she was in his mind's eye. Once out of the shapeless gown, her beauty became even more evident. A purist might say that she was slightly too buxom, but Alex was not a purist.

Later, as Alex and his companion returned to her apartment, he asked about the blonde.

She laughed a deep-throated sound. "Alex, love, I'd be jealous, except that I hear that she doesn't like men."

He cocked an eyebrow disbelievingly. "You mean . . . ?"

She interrupted with another laugh. "No, I just mean that she doesn't see anyone. Don't you know anything about her?"

He shook his head and she continued as though reciting.

"Amanda Lowell Adams, great, great, great, et cetera, granddaughter of presidents, Supreme Court justices, governors, you name it. A real blue blood. Pure Boston aristocracy. I'm surprised you haven't heard of her. Jack signed her for the film straight out of Yale Drama School."

He digested that. It fit. There was a quality about her—the kind of woman who could don a thrift shop rag, walk into a room full of women in designer originals, and outclass them all. He was intrigued.

Alex's thoughts strayed all too frequently that night to images of Amanda Adams.

"Dear, I simply do not understand why you insisted upon doing this." The slim gray-haired matron sat ramrod straight in the high-backed Chippendale chair. The expression on her still lovely features was one of distaste.

Across the handsomely furnished library, Amanda lowered her gaze, pretending interest in the crystal tumbler of fine old sherry in her hand. She stifled a sigh wondering just how many times she would have to justify her chosen vocation to her mother. From the time she had acted in her first play at the exclusive private school she had attended, she had known that acting would be her profession. When she had announced her intention following her first acclaimed performance, her family's reaction had been one of polite indulgence. It was not an uncommon dream for a young girl.

But for Amanda, the dream had persisted. She had accepted the piano and ballet lessons thrust upon her but had also insisted upon singing, acting and guitar lessons. The guitar lessons had caused a quarrel between Amanda and her parents. Only when she had stated flatly that she would find some way to earn the money to take them herself had they finally relented. But a guitar was simply not considered a suitable instrument for a well-bred young lady.

Her parents had always shown great interest in her progress in mastering the piano and ballet. They even came to accept the singing and acting lessons, but never once had they shown any interest whatever in her struggles with the guitar. Only Sam had encouraged her in this. Sam and Jay.

Her blue-eyed gaze strayed to those two, leaning casually against either side of the beautifully carved mantel of the well-used fireplace. How very dear they were to her. To even the most casual observer, there was a resemblance between Amanda and her brother Sam, despite his tall, athletic body and masculine features. There were five years between them, but they had always been very close.

The young man at the other end of the mantel seemed almost cut from the same mold—though his hair was darker. Jay Marshall was Sam's best friend and had always been another brother to Amanda, though she was well aware that he wanted to be much more than that now.

Amanda drew comfort from their presence —brother, friend, protectors both. That last was thrust into her mind as she recalled the previous evening.

But her mother seemed to be waiting for some kind of response, despite the fact that all this had been discussed before.

"Mother," she said evenly and calmly, "we have been over this before. I love acting. If I had enough volume to carry well on the stage, that would have been my first choice. But I don't, so I chose films."

Sam spoke up, sensing as always that she needed his assistance. "Mother, if you had seen Amanda perform, you would change your mind. Just look at those reviews—they tell the story. The critics are calling it an Academy Award performance." Sam gestured toward the pile of newspapers strewn across the baby grand piano in one corner of the large room.

Amanda allowed herself the luxury of a small smile. The critics had been kind—more than kind. All of them had hailed her as a major new star. It made the pain of her parents' rejection more acute.

She looked at her father, sitting quietly in a chair that matched the one in which his wife sat. Edward John Adams was a slim, patrician man, always impeccably dressed, quiet in manner. But she could sense his disapproval and disappointment. He had never actually said much about his daughter's choice of a career, deferring in such matters to his wife. But Amanda knew that he would prefer that she follow the accepted way of young women of her social class and do volunteer work for local charities. Any type of career would have been mildly disapproved of, but acting was simply unthinkable.

Jay spoke now, possibly to fill the uncomfortable silence that prevailed in the room.

"The critics weren't the only ones who liked Amanda. You should have seen the reaction of the crowd. I've never seen anything like it. She could have been visiting royalty." He shook his handsome head wonderingly.

Amanda winced. She wished that Jay had not mentioned that—partly because she knew it would upset her parents, and partly because it brought back too many unpleasant feelings.

"Really, Amanda, how could you possibly enjoy that kind of attention?" Her mother's disapproval was obvious now, and, out of the corner of her eye, Amanda saw Jay shoot her a look of apology.

"I don't enjoy it, Mother. But it goes with the work. There's no avoiding it." Her voice was the same as before. She wanted to change the subject.

Again Sam helped her. "So what's next, golden girl?" He gave her a slow smile, using the pet name that he and Jay had used since she was a little girl tagging after them.

Relieved at the change in conversation, Amanda relaxed somewhat.

"Next is rest. Sue and Rob have invited me to visit them in St. John's, and I plan to go there next week. It will be heaven—lying on the beach, doing absolutely nothing."

"Will you be doing another film, Amanda?" Her father's low voice broke into her reverie.

"Yes, Daddy, I will, but I have no immediate plans. My agent says he has several interesting offers, but I don't even want to look at any scripts right now." She gave her father a level look and was met by a troubled gaze.

Later that evening when Amanda had finally managed to escape to her spacious bedroom, she found that though she was tired, sleep eluded her. Forsaking her bed for the elegant velvet-covered chaise in one corner, she curled up contemplatively.

. She felt a strange mixture of satisfaction and fear. Satisfaction that a performance she had felt was excellent had been judged so by experts, and fear of the consequences of that acclaim. She was surprised

—and more than a little irritated with herself—that she should fear her success. After all, she had worked so hard to achieve it.

Part of the fear, she knew, could be blamed on her parents' disapproval. If that opposition could never be overcome (and privately, she suspected it never would be), she would just learn to live with it. Gloomily, she decided that it was certainly time she accepted that they were never going to be very happy with her.

But the other part of that fear was a different matter. She felt her anger rising. It was unfair. Was she to be haunted for the rest of her life by something that happened seven years ago?

She believed that she had resolutely put that night from her mind—but there it was again. The pain and shame she had felt were muted but the memory was all too clear.

The summer of her sixteenth year she had worked as a Counselor-in-Training at a girls' camp in Vermont. Her parents, always protective of their lovely daughter, had opposed it until Amanda's older cousin had accepted a counselor position at a nearby boys' camp. It was only then that they had felt she would be carefully watched over. It was ironic, to say the least, that this cousin had been indirectly responsible for what happened.

One evening Amanda had gone to see her cousin, armed with an interesting tidbit of family news that she had received in a letter from her mother. She had lingered longer than she had intended, and it was dusk as she set off for her own camp, following a well-marked path. Her cousin had volunteered to accompany her but she had refused, chafing at the thought that he was treating her like a child.

Her lovely mouth set grimly as she deliberately conjured up the scene. Lost in her thoughts, she had at first assumed that the male voices she heard were coming from the camp she had left behind. By the time she realized her mistake, she had come upon them. A group of five or six young men from a nearby town were visibly drunk, the result of a beer party in an isolated patch of woods.

She had initially felt only mild alarm when they spotted her and came toward her. Amanda had always had a great deal of confidence in her ability to handle herself, and she could not bring herself to think of them as a threat.

But then one of them said something she had never been able to recall. It had acted as a catalyst as they had surrounded her, grabbing at her roughly. She shuddered violently as she recalled their drunken fumbling. She heard again the sickening sound of her clothing being ripped from her, felt again those horrible hands touching her. For a long moment she had been too frozen with fear to struggle or cry out. But an instinct for self-preservation had surfaced quickly, and she had begun to struggle valiantly, while letting out a shriek that surprised even her own ears.

Although she knew that it had been only a few minutes, it had seemed like an eternity before she heard other voices, including that of her cousin, calling her name.

Even when the others arrived and quickly subdued

the drunken group, it was not over for her. Shame was as strong as fear had been. She recalled painfully how she had tried to cover her near-nakedness, and still remembered with gratitude how her cousin had quickly stripped off his shirt to cover her.

Amanda had been taken home immediately, bruised in mind and body. Recovery had been a slow, agonizing process, helped inestimably by a wise woman therapist.

Amanda forced herself to relax, wondering if she should go see that therapist again. Dorothy had become more of a friend and less of a therapist over the years, and Amanda was pleased to recall the large bouquet of flowers that had been delivered on opening night, with an encouraging note from Dorothy.

Amanda knew now that Dorothy had spoken several times with her parents and she was certain that they had been told to be less protective. But that advice, sound though it was, had fallen on deaf ears. Her parents had always been overly protective, and since they had undoubtedly blamed themselves for what had happened to her, they could not change.

For her part Amanda had at first welcomed their protection. But long after the incident had begun to recede into the depths of her memory, they had continued to make oblique references to it to justify their continued close watch over her and inadvertently keeping it fresh in her mind.

A silken cocoon had been spun about her and she had not resisted—although she was certainly aware of its existence. Now she began to sense the first tears in that gossamer webbing.

At the same time she knew that she still needed that protection. The evening of the New York premiere she had been hurried from the limousine into the theater between Sam and Jay. The crowds had not frightened her, until a particularly exuberant group of young men had almost succeeded in breaking through the police lines. Then, for just a moment, seven years had melted away, and once more she had felt terror.

2

Amanda sat with two men at a small table at "21."
One was her agent, Murray Weisman; the other, Peter
Ulanavich, the producer and director.

After they had ordered drinks Peter turned to
Amanda. "So you like the story?"

She nodded, her golden hair swinging. "Yes, I read
the book, and I think it will make a splendid film. The
role of Maggie would be a challenge for any actress."

Peter relaxed a bit. He had been afraid it might be
more difficult to persuade her. But he knew she was
perfect for the role. The combination of her delicate,
patrician beauty and her proven ability to play a
strong role would be exactly right for his next film.

"If I hadn't seen that videotape of your performance in that avant-garde thing at Yale, I might never
have believed that you could handle a role like this."
He paused as the drinks arrived.

"Of course, there was a certain inner strength in your character in 'The Winds of Change,' but the role of Maggie will be much more demanding, quite apart from the aging. Have you ever done anything that required you to age?"

Amanda- nodded. "Yes, but only in school. Of course, I know that there's quite a lot more to it than just makeup tricks."

Peter nodded his agreement and continued to talk enthusiastically about the film. At one point the conversation shifted to the business of money, with Murray smoothly taking over while Amanda sat silently. She really didn't like this part of the conversation, and as her gaze roamed about the elegant, high-ceilinged room, decided that it was a very good thing for her that she had Murray. She tended to get quite caught up in her enthusiasm for a role and would have taken the part for very little.

Murray was arguing persuasively for a percentage of the gross, while Peter was balking that such deals were generally given only to established stars, and that Amanda did not yet qualify for that status. Murray snorted derisively, pointing out that an Academy Award nomination certainly proved her to be an established star. Everyone knew that the well-timed announcement of the retirement of an aging dramatic star had been the only reason Amanda had not won.

Peter didn't dispute this, but countered that there were those who thought that Amanda was a lightweight capable only of a simpler role such as that in "The Winds of Change." He didn't agree, obviously, but those who did would be hard to convince, and therefore her value to the film was not as great as that of an already established actress.

Amanda fidgeted uncomfortably as the two men continued to argue, both obviously enjoying themselves and oblivious of her for the moment. She hated being discussed like this. It was extremely distasteful and left her inclined to agree with her parents that films were a tawdry business.

Her parents had taken her decision to continue in films just as she had expected. Her father had met the announcement with stony silence, and her mother had expressed her earlier thoughts on the subject once again. There had been no shouting, of course—just quiet disapproval and fears for her peace of mind.

Sam was another matter altogether. He had been pleased, as she had also expected. His unwavering support of her made him all the dearer to her.

And then there was Jay, who fell somewhere in between. Like Sam, he had originally encouraged her. But now she felt his support wavering, and knew that he suspected she was slipping away from him forever. A sadness began to wash over her as she was drawn sharply from her thoughts.

"Amanda, you can come back to us now. The dirty business is over." It was Murray's voice that drew her back.

He looked at Peter and smiled broadly. "I tell you, Peter, she's the easiest client I've ever had. Whatever I say is okay with her."

Peter looked once again at the lovely vision seated across from him, wondering if she were really strong enough for this business. Amanda Adams was certainly unlike any other actress he had ever met. He wondered how long that seemingly genuine innocence would survive.

Peter Ulanavich continued to ponder that thought after he had parted from her and returned to his hotel. A good day's work had been done.

He had bought the film rights to "A Texas Odyssey" after his wife had persuaded him to read the book just as it was becoming a best-seller. It had taken everything he could scrape together to get it.

Then the problems had begun. Peter was an independent producer without major studio backing. His previous backers were somewhat wary this time. Peter's last two films had barely managed to recover their investments. Word had it that after an earlier string of successes, Peter was burned out. But the best-seller status of the book had attracted some smaller investors. And while he did not admit it to Murray, the fact that he was in negotiations to get Amanda for the starring role had also drawn some of the money. His investors knew that even if she bombed in the role, she would guarantee a good box office.

But he was still five million dollars short when he had run into Alex Wojyclas at a party. The thought of his principal backer propelled Peter to the phone. Peter knew he would want to hear that all the principals had now been signed.

Alex Wojyclas replaced the telephone receiver with a satisfied smile. He tilted back the big leather chair and allowed himself a moment to savor this welcome news.

Abruptly, he swung the chair around to gaze out unseeing at the mid-Manhattan skyline spread before him He ran a big hand absently through the already rumpled black hair that was just beginning to show traces of gray.

He was slightly troubled at the impetuous nature of what he had done. In the months since he had first seen Amanda Adams' face, and the party at which he had committed himself to backing "A Texas Odyssey," he had thought about her often. And that in itself was unusual for a man who thought very little about women—except for the obvious needs they satisfied.

At thirty-eight Alex Wojyclas was a millionaire many times over, both respected and feared in the highest echelons of American and international business. There was a quality of ruthless determination about him that, combined with his impressive physical stature, made him a formidable figure.

A smile played once again about his strong mouth as he silently congratulated himself on his suggestion to Peter that he give a party for the cast prior to the beginning of filming. He only hoped that she would come.

Amanda took note of the stares she was receiving as she checked into the Plaza, following the brief flight from Boston to New York. She was always recognized now. Between "The Winds of Change" and her record album, and, of course, the poster, she was truly a celebrity.

The poster was something she rather regretted despite, or perhaps because of, its success. Murray had talked her into it, and she had finally agreed after deciding to donate the proceeds to several charities. And it had turned out to be such a success that the coffers of those charities were rapidly filling.

It was scarcely risqué. She had immediately vetoed the suggestion that she wear a bikini and had finally been photographed in denim cut-offs and an open-necked shirt tied around her midriff. She was standing on a beach with one slim leg poised on a rock and a breeze blowing through her long hair. She had been aghast at the amount of time that had gone into the creation of such a simple photograph. But the results had apparently been worth the effort, since the poster had sold phenomenally well.

Two hours after her arrival, she stood staring at that now famous face and figure in the long mirror in her room. She was not happy to be here.

When Peter had called her about the party, she had at first declined. But he had been gently persuasive. Their host was his principal backer, and he needed to stay in the man's good graces because he expected to go over budget. Amanda liked Peter and finally agreed to please him. Besides, she had told herself it would be a good idea to meet the people with whom she would be sharing such an isolated life. They would be filming for several months in rural Texas and it was important that she be able to get along well with the other cast members. In many ways Amanda still felt herself an outsider to the business.

She looked at her reflection critically. The brilliant

blue gown accentuated her large blue eyes, and the top floated and draped over her slim shoulders while plunging to a deep vee that was more revealing than anything she usually wore. It had been the color rather than the style that had appealed to her. The dress was gathered at the waist by a gold chain belt, then fell straight to the floor, with a thigh-high slit.

Her only jewelry was a delicate gold chain, studded with tiny diamonds—a gift the previous Christmas from Jay.

How she wished that Jay might have accompanied her. But the party coincided with a family celebration that he was obligated to attend.

Reluctantly she picked up her small gold evening bag and a white crocheted shawl—handmade by her grandmother—and hurried from the room to meet the car that her host had insisted on providing.

She was once more conscious of stares as she hurried through the marble-pillared lobby, under the crystal chandelier, and over the lovely oriental rug. She paused before she descended the stairs, noting the long gray Rolls parked outside.

At her appearance the uniformed chauffeur straightened up from where he had been lounging against the hood of the car and approached her, touching his cap lightly. "Good evening, Miss Adams."

She smiled at the greeting and slid gracefully onto the leather seat, settling back into the deeply cushioned upholstery as the car moved out into traffic.

Her thoughts turned to her host. Peter had told her that he was the film's principal backer and president of CRI. She hadn't known what that was at the time, but had recalled later that she had heard her brother and Jay mention the company. She had mentioned it to Sam.

"Alex Wojyclas?" Sam hadn't even stumbled over the name as she had. "I have heard it said that he has an interest in actresses, but I didn't know that he backed films," Sam threw her an amused look.

"CRI is a conglomerate—mining mostly. It's grown very quickly the past few years."

"Do you know Alex Wojyclas?" Amanda was curious.

"Only by reputation. He's a Stanford man—won a Heisman playing football for them. I believe Ruskowski, the company's founder, hired him straight out of school. He inherited control of the company when Ruskowski died. Brilliant man, I understand. Inclined to be somewhat ruthless on occasion, but I suppose that's necessary." That was all he had said, but she had sensed her brother's disapproval of the man.

The Rolls glided to a stop in front of an imposing new building. The chauffeur helped her out, and the doorman tipped his hat to her.

"Good evening, Miss Adams. Just take the elevator to your left."

Amanda did as told, noting that it was obviously a private elevator. Once again she wished that she were elsewhere.

The door slid noiselessly open onto a small, starkly modern foyer decorated with abstract sculpture and large plants under concealed lighting. A doorway opposite the elevator opened as she hesitantly approached it.

Only years of careful social training prevented a gasp from escaping her lips. He was in black tie—impeccably tailored. But even so, it did not seem right. Such a man belonged in a plaid shirt and worn jeans. He was very tall and powerfully built with a rumpled thatch of jet black hair. His face was devastatingly masculine, rather than classically handsome—square-jawed with a deep cleft in the chin, and a wide mouth beneath a straight nose that was slightly marred by a small bump. Something inside her reacted involuntarily to the aura of barely leashed power about him. The gray eyes that looked down at her sent fingers of fire and ice coursing through her.

"Good evening, Amanda. Come in, please." It was a deep voice, a voice that commanded rather than requested. And she thought immediately that it suited him well.

She became aware of the sounds of the party drifting out from behind him, and flashing him her best social smile passed close beside him. At that moment she was jolted by a sudden awareness of him, a primeval recognition of the words "male" and "female." Never had the two seemed so totally opposite to her.

"I'm Alex Wojyclas," he said unnecessarily, and she automatically extended a hand, which was clasped by a huge, calloused hand that sent further shock waves through her. She was at once aware that all the other men she knew had much softer hands. She was eye level with his broad chest and tipped back her head slowly, looking up at him under long lashes.

Gray eyes met blue, and for a moment the world vanished.

"Let me take that for you." She flinched as he touched her shoulders lightly, removing the shawl without waiting for her assent.

Amanda stood rooted in place for a moment. Where was all her self-assurance? Later she would attempt to rationalize her reaction to him. But for the moment, she could only wonder at the strength of that reaction.

However, when his hand lightly touched her back urging her into the room where the party appeared to be in full swing, she managed to throw him a quick sidelong glance that quite clearly indicated her displeasure.

"Amanda, there you are." She turned in relieved gratitude at the sound of Peter's voice as he approached.

She was quickly introduced to the others by the gregarious director. Alex had left her side after inquiring what she would like to drink. Her gaze lingered on his broad back for some seconds before she turned her attention to the others.

He returned accompanied by a stunning redhead whom Amanda recognized immediately as the actress Laura Shannon. Perhaps, thought Amanda unkindly, the word "actress" was not quite appropriate, since Laura's success in films owed far less to ability than to her truly astonishing physical attributes.

When Alex introduced the two women it took very little perception on Amanda's part to guess that Laura did not like her. And from the way she clung to Alex it also seemed obvious that she regarded him as her personal property.

She was actually grateful when their host excused himself once again to greet some other guests, accompanied, of course, by the seductive Laura. But, even when he was not at her side, Amanda found that her gaze was drawn involuntarily to him to find those gray eyes returning her stare. It was unnerving. Finally, in a gesture she knew to be rude, she quite deliberately turned her back on him and joined a spirited discussion of the trials and tribulations of working on location.

Sometime later she moved away from the group and hurried off to the small panelled study she had noticed earlier. She simply had to get some quiet for a few minutes.

The door stood half ajar and she stepped in, halting abruptly as she saw him seated at the desk with one hand on the phone.

"Oh, I'm sorry. I didn't mean to intrude." She stumbled over her words and felt her face flush warmly.

"You're not intruding. Come in, Amanda," Alex Wojyclas said softly.

There was something in his tone that troubled her—and definitely something in those steely eyes that roved slowly over her. She hesitated.

"I . . . I was just looking for someplace quiet." The words almost tumbled out, and she felt a totally unaccustomed awkwardness in the overpowering presence of this man.

He unfolded his long frame from the chair and waved toward a couch.

"Be my guest. I'm finished with the call."

He came toward her, and her pulse began to race, pounding loudly in her ears.

He stopped quite close to her, and before she could move past him, his hand suddenly moved, resting lightly against the soft curve where her neck met her shoulders, a hard thumb pressing against the pulse point at the base of her throat.

"Is that from fear, or . . . ?" He left the sentence unfinished as she unwillingly raised her eyes to meet his.

She grabbed at his hand to force it away, but he dropped it willingly, a knowing smile curving his wide mouth. Before she could formulate some response, he turned and left the room.

When Amanda finally returned to the party, the first thing she saw was Alex deep in conversation with Dack Temple, her costar in the film. At forty-two, Dack was one of the top male box office stars—tall, blond and rugged. But Amanda could not help thinking that even Dack Temple was no match for Alex Wojyclas. As that gray-eyed gaze swept once more over her, she turned abruptly and went off to find Peter.

"Well, what do you think of our host?" Peter cast a dark-eyed glance at the man across the room from them.

"He's very . . . impressive." She hesitated over her choice of words.

Peter laughed. "Quite. You know, I've met some big-business types before, but I've never met one like him. Talk about an aura of power." He paused, shaking his head slowly. "I'd hate to cross him."

Amanda nodded in agreement, feeling somewhat relieved to learn that her impression had not been such a personal one after all.

Dack Temple proved to be a charming companion, and an instant rapport sprang up between them. Amanda was very glad about that since they would be working closely together. He was remarkably free of the egotism that was usually present in top stars. Amanda had often read about him in the papers. It appeared that he usually eschewed the Hollywood scene. About a year ago he had lost his wife of almost twenty years to cancer and was left with two teenaged children. Amanda appreciated his company and found his calm steadiness very soothing to her rattled nerves.

Sometime later she once again escaped from the party briefly and went out onto the broad terrace that opened off the large living room. The nighttime noises of the great city were muted in the distance, and a light breeze sprang up, blowing through her long hair. She shivered slightly at the coolness.

And then she felt her shawl being draped across her shoulders by large hands that were becoming all too familiar. She jumped. She had thought he was well-occupied with Laura Shannon.

"I thought you might be cold out here." The deep voice came from close behind her.

She moved quickly away from him and cast a frosty glance over her shoulder. "Thank you. That was very thoughtful of you." Her tone was icy.

A slight smile played across the strong features. "Just protecting my investment." She had the sudden impression that the words, however lightly spoken, had a deeper meaning.

Before she could think of a reply, he asked, "Will you have dinner with me tomorrow evening, Amanda?"

The sudden shift in conversation caught her off guard, but she replied evenly enough. "I'm afraid I can't. I must go back to Boston tomorrow. I have an engagement tomorrow night." That was true, thank goodness. She gave him a politely regretful smile, certain that would be the end of that conversation.

"I see. Then perhaps the following evening—in Boston?"

This question once again caught her unprepared. It did cross her mind that he was, after all, the film's principal backer, and she recalled Peter's concern about staying in his good graces. So she found herself nodding her acceptance and making the arrangements, although with obviously limited enthusiasm. But he seemed not to notice, she noted irritably.

"What did you say his name is, dear?" Amanda recognized her mother's question for what it actually was—a fervent plea that she had not heard correctly.

Before she could repeat the name, her father spoke up. "Wojyclas? You mean the head of CRI?" The only thing she could detect in her father's tone was surprise.

She turned to him, trying to ignore her mother for

the moment. She had been hoping they would be out for the evening and she would be spared this. She again thought about moving into her own apartment.

"Yes, Daddy. He's the principal backer of the film. It was his party I went to in New York two nights ago. That's when I met him. You've heard of him?" She noted that her father had had no trouble with the difficult name.

"Of course." Although he seemed about to continue, he was prevented from doing so by the appearance of the housekeeper in the open doorway of the library. The subject of their conversation loomed behind her.

Amanda rose quickly and extended her hand graciously. "Alex, you're very prompt. I'd like you to meet my parents." She turned and introduced him first to her mother, who managed a few polite words. Amanda was certain that he was unaware of her mother's disapproval—only someone who knew her as well as her daughter would have seen it.

She then introduced her father, whose interest was undisguised. While Amanda wasn't at all certain that he approved of Alex as a suitable escort for his daughter, it was apparent that his interest in Alex's business momentarily took precedence over any disapproval. When Alex agreed to stay for a drink, they entered quickly into a discussion of some recent CRI acquisition.

Amanda resumed her seat and cast a quick glance at her mother, who was poised on the very edge of her chair, ready to fly into the conversation at the slightest hesitation on the part of the two men.

"Are you from New York originally, Mr. Wojyclas?" Amanda heard the polite question insert itself into a momentary lull. In the past Amanda had occasionally brought people home whom she felt she had to protect from her mother's genteel inquisition. She felt no such compunction now. In fact, she thought wickedly, she might almost enjoy seeing Alex squirm—if indeed he did. She turned to see him give her mother a polite smile.

"No, Mrs. Adams, I'm originally from Wyoming." He hesitated for just a fraction of a second, and Amanda would have sworn that she saw the ghost of a smile cross his face as he continued.

"My father was an immigrant miner from Poland, and the family settled there."

Amanda digested this bit of information as she watched for her mother's reaction. "I see," was the only response she could give, and Amanda was surprised to see Alex save her from further embarrassment—or was he merely forestalling further questioning?—by standing and approaching Amanda.

"I've made reservations for dinner, and I think we had better be leaving now."

Though Amanda could not in all truthfulness have said that Alex appeared uncomfortable in the presence of her parents, she sensed, or thought she sensed, a certain stiffness in him as they left the house. Secretly she had to admit that it didn't bother her very much. She felt that she had been forced into accepting this date with him, suspecting that he was well aware of his power as the film's chief backer and not at all averse to using that power. That being the case, she felt justified in using any "weapon" at her disposal.

To her surprise, the restaurant he had selected was one of her favorites. She wondered how he had known about it, since it was small and not particularly well known outside certain select Boston circles.

The maitre d' had greeted her warmly and Alex deferentially. She noted uncomfortably the politely surprised looks she had received from several people who knew her. Amanda was very rarely seen with men other than her relatives and Jay.

When he asked her for a recommendation from the small menu, she forced herself to concentrate on it, all the while aware of his gray-eyed scrutiny. He did make her uncomfortable.

She finally raised her eyes to meet his, though she found it surprisingly difficult. "They're famous for their seafood, particularly the scrod. You might want to try that or perhaps the *truite à bleu.*"

She saw a slight frown cross his face, accompanied by a brief narrowing of the eyes that seemed locked upon her. But it was quickly gone, and she couldn't imagine the cause.

They ordered and sat sipping their drinks as they waited for dinner to arrive. He asked her about the upcoming film, and that led into a discussion about acting. He was a good listener, she noticed, and seemed to have a strong working knowledge of the film industry. She recalled what Sam had said about his having an interest in actresses.

As she began to talk about her profession, she relaxed somewhat. However, an indefinable tension remained between them, and she suddenly wondered if he just might be as uncomfortable with her as she was with him. It was a strange thought. After his overly familiar behavior of the other evening, it was difficult to imagine him being ill at ease with her now. But the impression lingered.

Over after-dinner drinks, Amanda asked him about himself.

"As I said, I grew up in Wyoming. I won a football scholarship to Stanford and went to work for CRI right after law school."

Amanda recalled that Sam had mentioned that he had been a very good football player. Something about a trophy?

Aloud she said, "I understand that you were a very good football player. My brother said you won? . . ." she gestured helplessly, unable to recall its name.

"The Heisman Trophy. Yes, I did. One of the big decisions I had to make at that point was whether or not to go pro. I decided on law school instead."

Amanda thought about that. "I suppose that professional football must be very different from college football. I mean it really isn't a game then, is it?"

He shrugged his wide shoulders. "It's not so different. At least it wouldn't have been for me. In essence I was paid to play football in college. If I had been seriously injured, or if I hadn't played well, the pay, in the form of the scholarship, would have stopped." He paused and gave her a look that sent an unaccountable chill through her.

"In any event, I play to win regardless of the game."

Amanda shuddered inwardly at the hardness his

words implied. Was he issuing a warning to her? When he took her home, she felt compelled to invite him in, all the while hoping that he would decline the invitation. But she quickly learned that he did not seem to recognize a politely meaningless invitation. Or perhaps he did recognize it but chose to accept anyway. In any event she left him in the elegant living room and went off to make coffee.

When she returned with the coffee service, he was bent over, examining the spinning wheel in one corner of the room.

"That belonged to my great-great-grandmother. Some of her handiwork still survives. I'm afraid that it's purely decorative now. Neither my mother nor I have ever learned to use it."

He turned to face her as she set down the antique silver coffee service, and she glanced up at him to find him regarding her with a strange expression. It crossed her mind that this man actually disliked her. It was only a fleeting impression, of course, but a strong one nonetheless.

They settled themselves on either end of the velvet-covered Chippendale sofa after she had poured coffee.

"How does your family feel about your career?" The tone of his question implied that he already knew the answer to that one.

Amanda shrugged lightly and raised the delicate Aynsley cup to her lips. "Naturally, they're not very happy about it. But they know that it's what I want." She threw a rather defiant look at him as though daring him to contradict her.

"Naturally," he repeated drily, picking up his own cup somewhat gingerly. "But I'm sure they would be much happier if you contented yourself with doing charity work."

That dry tone and the truth of his statement began to anger her. She sat rigidly at her end of the sofa, unconsciously mimicking the posture her mother always assumed in distasteful situations.

But she replied evenly enough. "I'm sure they would. But, as I said, it's my choice."

"Why is it your choice, Amanda? Somehow, I don't quite see you as a rebel."

A small smile played about the corners of her mouth at his remark, so much like one made by her father some years earlier. And her reply was much the same.

She turned to him. "There have been other rebels in my family, you know. In fact one could say that it's a family tradition."

He caught her inference, nodding slightly, with an amused look. "But it's only a temporary condition, I'm sure. Once you've had your fill, you will return to the fold."

She bristled at his remark. "Acting is my career, Alex. I intend to work at it as long as I'm able."

To her great relief he said no more on the subject. And she was even more relieved when he rose to leave. She followed him to the door.

He stood there for a moment, looking down at her. As she raised her eyes to meet his, for just a brief second she found herself wondering what it would be like to be in his arms. She began to flush warmly and lowered her head to hide the evidence.

But his hand suddenly reached out to cup her chin and pull it up. One finger slowly traced the outline of her face.

"You're very beautiful, Amanda. Too beautiful." The hand dropped. "I'll be out of the country for a while and very busy after that. But I'll be in touch as soon as I can." And after a brief good night he was gone, leaving her standing there in a state of shock.

There had been no question about whether or not she would see him again. He had just assumed that she would. It was a while before she could summon up righteous anger.

As she prepared for bed, Amanda was sure of only one thing—she had no intention of seeing him again. She would be leaving for California in a week for some prefilm work and studio shooting. After that they would be off on location in rural Texas.

But she was not yet allowed to put Alex Wojyclas from her mind. Her mother brought up the subject the next morning at breakfast.

"Where did you go for dinner last night, dear?"

Amanda told her and was rewarded with a faint grimace.

"Now why ever did he take you there, of all places? And I suppose that there must have been people there who know you."

"Mother, really!" Amanda spoke rather more sharply than she intended. "You make it sound as though I should have been ashamed of being seen with him. He's the head of a very large corporation after all. That hardly makes him a disreputable character."

Faced with her daughter's sarcasm, Harriet Adams continued calmly. "I didn't say he was disreputable. And he is attractive in a coarse kind of way, I suppose." It was a bone tossed gratuitously to soothe her fractious daughter. "It's just that I'm concerned about the kind of people you will be associating with if you continue in the film business."

"I doubt very much that I will be seeing him again, Mother. And as to others like him, I can certainly work with people like that without associating with them socially." Even as she spoke the words, Amanda was privately of the opinion that it was highly unlikely she would find anyone quite like Alex—in or out of the film industry.

3

~~~~~~~~~~

Amanda sat uncomfortably in the artificial shade of a large beach umbrella and watched her fellow actors working on a scene that was in its seventh take. She was very glad to be out of this one since it looked as though many more takes were ahead.

Late summer in Texas was not the most desirable season, but the realism demanded by Peter required that they be here at this time. The land was dry and brown, except for the purplish hills rising in the distance. And the sun was brutal. Amanda had already acquired a light tan—as much as the makeup crew would permit.

As Peter signalled for a break, she scrambled to her feet and went over to him.

"Peter, do you think you'll be needing me again today?" She fervently hoped not because she wanted nothing more than to escape to the seedy little motel, whose one redeeming quality was that it had air conditioning.

He turned to her, exasperation plain on his perspiring face. "I seriously doubt it. The way this is going I may not need you tomorrow either." He cast a baleful glance at her leading man as he approached them. Before turning his attention to Dack Temple, Peter told her to go ahead and leave for the day.

They were using Jeeps for transportation, and Amanda found one of the drivers, who was more than happy to escape his boredom and drive her back.

After a dusty and bumpy ride back to the main highway, they sped along in the noisy little vehicle until they reached the outskirts of town. He turned in at the "Tumbleweed Motel," and she wondered once again what it was doing here. It almost seemed as though it had been created expressly for their use— except that it had obviously been built a very long time ago. They reasoned that it was used by the extra cowhands hired by area ranchers at roundup time.

The driver dropped her at her door and waved good-bye as he swung around toward the other end of the motel, where he undoubtedly would head for the bar and wait in air-conditioned comfort before returning later for the others.

She had just entered the sparsely furnished little room, blessing its coolness, when the phone rang.

"Miss Adams? It's Jerry, at the desk. I saw you come in. There's a message here for you. Want to pick it up, or should I read it to you?"

Amanda frowned. She really didn't want to walk all the way down there for the message—and anyway, he would already have read it.

"Thank you, Jerry. Please read it to me."

"Right. I've got it right here." He paused for a few seconds. "It says: 'Be at the landing strip at 5:30 tomorrow. Will pick you up there. Dinner in Dallas.' And it's from an Alex." His voice told her that he was smirking.

Amanda was dumbfounded. She stared in astonishment at the phone receiver as though it were somehow lying to her. Finally she thanked Jerry politely and hung up. Then she sat down on the edge of the bed and continued to stare at the phone.

How dare he leave such a message? Determined to show him that she could not be ordered around, she picked up the phone and then hurriedly put it down again.

Amanda suspected that Jerry could quite easily listen in on their calls. And since she suspected that he had an interest in her, she was quite sure he would do just that. Angry as she was with Alex, she had no desire to provide entertainment for anyone. Besides, she reasoned, if he was planning to meet her in Dallas tomorrow, he might not be in New York at all— although his secretary would surely know where to find him.

The only alternative she could see was to get to a public phone. There was one in the bar, but at this time of day it would be filled with the usual assortment of rough-looking cowboys. Furthermore, she had no desire to go back out into the stifling heat.

As the first wave of anger subsided, and logic prevailed, Amanda decided there was really no reason she should attempt to contact him. Her answer would be quite simply not to show up at the airstrip. Let the pilot sit and wait. He would surely give up at some point and leave. It would serve Alex right to pay unnecessarily for the pilot and plane. Yes, she liked the idea very much. Amanda was not a vindictive person, but she suspected that if he continued to bother her she could very easily become one.

She clenched her fists tightly as she recalled the last time she had seen him. Peter and his wife, Jan, had talked her into accompanying them to a party saying that she had to go to at least one Hollywood party. She had been there for two weeks working very hard and finally agreed that it might be an amusing diversion.

But it had scarcely been that. She had felt out of place from the very beginning, despite Peter and Jan's efforts to see that she met as many of the people as possible. Amanda had never been to a party like this. The liquor was flowing altogether too freely, and the women present were showing so much bare skin that Amanda felt positively Victorian in her modestly cut violet sundress.

Then Alex appeared with the sultry Laura Shannon clinging to his arm. Amanda was forced to exchange some social pleasantries with them and endure Laura's pointed remark that she was surprised to see Amanda there—an obvious statement that Amanda was very much out of her element, while she, Laura Shannon, was very much in hers. Amanda, casting a brief glance at the barely covered voluptuous curves of the other woman, decided she was right—and welcome to it.

Alex's presence only increased her sense of discomfort and she finally decided to escape for a few minutes to a secluded part of the big terrace behind the sprawling house. It was still too early to make her excuses to their host, a famous producer to whom Peter owed his start in the business.

Amanda had been standing there for only a few minutes, half hidden by large concrete planters, when a voice cut into her thoughts. "Ah, there you are, Amanda. I've been looking all over for you."

Amanda recognized with a wave of disgust the slightly slurred tones of a handsome young man named Chuck, who had been bothering her at every opportunity. Indeed, he was one of the reasons she had chosen to escape from the party. Jan had told her that he was the current lover of an aging film star who had a predilection for young Adonis types.

Amanda shuddered as she recalled how he had grabbed her, pressing his mouth to the cheek she had turned to avoid his kiss. But before she could push him away, another voice intruded on the scene.

"Chuck, I think Desiree is looking for you." There was no mistaking the note of dry amusement in Alex's deep voice. For a moment Amanda had been afraid that Chuck would make a scene, but finally, either from fear of Alex or fear of Desiree's wrath, he released her and left.

Amanda gave Alex a heartfelt smile of gratitude and

could not resist asking if Desiree were really looking for him.

"Hardly. The last time I saw her she was trying to seduce someone else's boyfriend."

But her gratitude vanished when she learned that Peter had sent Alex out after her. It seemed that Peter had noticed both Amanda's and Chuck's exits and was about to intervene himself, when he caught sight of a new arrival he wanted to speak to. So he asked Alex to check on her.

Instead of being grateful for their concern, Amanda had become angry at the assumption that she could not take care of herself. She thanked him again and turned to go back into the house. But a long arm shot out to detain her—a slight pressure on her arm, his hard fingers pressing against her soft skin.

"So you haven't yet had your fill of all this?" He waved negligently about them with his free arm.

Amanda made no reply and he continued. "Amanda, if you had any sense at all, you would pack up and go back where you belong."

Her gratitude toward him completely forgotten now, she glared at him. "Thanks for the advice, Alex, but I really can take care of myself. And, as I told you, acting is my career."

A muscle flexed slightly along the strong jaw as he looked down at her.

"I wonder just how long you will be able to manage the balancing act, Amanda."

Her puzzled frown drew an immediate response. "The virginal socialite and the sex symbol."

Amanda flushed at his remark, but she replied icily, "You just could be wrong in your assumptions, Alex." She regretted the words as soon as they were out of her mouth.

Both dark brows rose quickly. "Could I now? If so, that raises some interesting possibilities." And the long look he had given her before she turned on her heel had been frankly assessing.

Amanda grimaced as she recalled the conversation all too clearly. Why had she allowed him to bait her like that? And why, after not bothering her for all these weeks, was he suddenly thrusting himself into her life again? She decided that her failure to keep the date would certainly be sufficiently clear notice that she wanted nothing more to do with him.

Midway through the next day, Amanda had almost forgotten about Alex's message. And she had certainly forgotten her slightly smug attitude of the day before, watching her fellow actors do the same scene over and over.

She had believed rather foolishly that the scene she was working on would be relatively easy. She and Dack had gone over it briefly the evening before, and both of them had been satisfied with the results.

But Peter had not been at all satisfied. Amanda could only be grateful that he wasn't the kind of director who raged and screamed at his players.

The first part of the scene had gone nicely, despite a minor mishap. The script called for Amanda, a newly arrived Eastern bride, to ride out through the empty land to bring a surprise picnic lunch to her rancher husband played by Dack.

While she was riding across the open land, along-side two Jeeps loaded with camera equipment, tech-nicians and the Assistant Director, one of the Jeeps struck a hidden rock, and camera and cameraman had almost been thrown out of the Jeep. Unfortunately, the camera involved was the one in use at the moment, and they had all been forced to back up some distance and, after much good-natured joking, start over again.

Amanda had actually enjoyed the scene at first, since she loved to ride—especially after she had gotten used to the comfort of the big Western saddle. She had ridden all her life but strictly English style. Peter had declared that to be a bonus since the woman she portrayed would also have ridden English, if at all, before coming out West.

But from then on it had all been downhill. Peter hadn't been satisfied with the scene in which Amanda has an angry confrontation with her older husband, who criticizes her for riding alone and turning a busy workday into a frivolous picnic.

By the time the scene was finally shot to Peter's satisfaction, Amanda was feeling as irritable as the character she portrayed. She couldn't help wondering if that was exactly what Peter had intended.

As she stripped off the jeans and tee shirt back in her motel room, she suddenly recalled the date with Alex. A quick glance at her clock told her that the pilot sent for her would have been cooling his heels at the strip for over half an hour now. Although she felt sorry for him, she certainly felt no guilt about standing up Alex. He definitely deserved it. She was just a little nervous about what he might do, but guessed he would do no more than call her at some point and then leave her alone.

She stayed in the shower a long time, washing away the day's accumulation of dirt and perspiration. Films are such a glamorous business, she thought grimly. If the public only knew.

Finally satisfied that she was clean, she stepped out of the shower, wrapped one towel around her wet hair and another around her slim body, and went to get the soda she had left on a table in the small room.

A gasp escaped her as she saw Alex sitting there casually leafing through a magazine.

"Wh . . . what are you doing here?"

His steely gaze swept over her scantily clad figure, lingering at the spot where she clutched the towel at the top and the soft swell of her full breasts fluttered with her agitated breathing.

"We had a date, remember?" There was a trace of sarcasm in his voice.

"I . . . we worked late," she said by way of explanation. That was true, but she wondered why she suddenly lacked the courage to tell him that she had no intention of keeping the date.

He stood up and stretched his long frame. She had not moved.

"By the way I did knock, but you obviously didn't hear me because of the shower. Since the door was unlocked, I came in." He regarded her thoughtfully. "I would suggest that you keep your door locked, Amanda. Not every man would be as much of a gentleman as I'm being."

While there was certainly truth in what he said, his patronizing tone snapped the last remaining shred of pleasantry she could muster.

"Gentleman? I don't call it gentlemanly to order someone to have dinner with you. I've always been led to believe that gentlemen *asked* for dates." She drew herself up haughtily and tried to achieve some semblance of dignity. It was, however, rather difficult with her wrapped in a towel and him towering over her.

Gray eyes narrowed on her with amusement. "I don't recall that I said I was a gentleman all the time."

Then he turned away from her abruptly. "Get dressed while I find some way of transporting us back to the plane."

Amanda glared at his broad back. "I will not get dressed. And for your information, Alex, I had no intention of meeting that plane. I will not be ordered about." Her final words tapered off in volume as he turned back to her.

This time he made a quite deliberate slow sweep of her—from head to toe. She felt her face flush hotly.

"Very well. Don't get dressed. It could be a more interesting evening here that way." His tone was suggestive, and Amanda knew that she had turned beet red.

He laughed then and resumed his intentions toward the phone.

"Get me Peter Ulanavich." A pause. "Peter, it's Alex. I'm in Amanda's room. I have a plane at the landing strip, and we're going to Dallas for dinner. Since you kept her late today, could you manage without her tomorrow morning?" Another brief pause. "Fine. I'll have her back by noon." He turned briefly to glance at Amanda who hadn't moved.

"Will you go get some clothes on?" he said to Amanda. "Peter, could you find someone to drive us back to the strip? I hitched a ride with a local. Thanks." He hung up and turned back to find her disappearing into the bathroom.

His laughter followed her. She slammed the door and leaned against it shaking. He had deliberately sought to humiliate her in front of Peter. And what was she to do about it? She didn't want to involve Peter in this, since it would put him in a very difficult situation with Alex.

A tap on the door roused her from her thoughts, and without thinking, she pulled it open. He stood there holding one of her dresses.

"I like this. Pink is a good color for blushing blondes." There was no mistaking the amusement he was gaining at her expense. She grabbed the dress from him and flung it toward the bed where it slithered to the floor in a heap.

"I am not going with you. And how can you tell Peter that I'll take tomorrow morning off? Time is money, and they need me tomorrow morning." Her voice rose with each word.

He remained unperturbed. "Exactly. And it's my money. Or had you forgotten that?"

"That doesn't give you the right to my company whenever you choose. That was not in my contract." She silently congratulated herself on her sarcasm.

"Perhaps not, but you would like to see this film

completed, wouldn't you?" There was a softly menacing quality to his voice.

"If I were to pull out at some point Peter would have one hell of a time getting anyone else to invest."

Amanda's mouth dropped open in astonishment. "You wouldn't." She almost choked on her words. "Do you mean to tell me that if I don't go out with you, you would allow this film to be scrapped?" She was incredulous.

He shrugged his wide shoulders. "I really don't know. Let's both hope that we don't have to find out. Now, for the last time, will you get dressed and pack a bag for overnight? Or do we spend the evening here? I have only so much control, you know, and I'm afraid that spending an evening in a motel room with America's latest sex symbol wrapped in a towel just might be more than I can handle."

When she did not respond, he took a step toward her and she was involuntarily galvanized into movement. Without a word, she picked up the pink dress and hung it back in the closet, selecting instead a blue printed dress. Then she gathered her other clothes and retreated once again to the bathroom.

She dressed mechanically as she strove to regain control of herself and wondered if he would really carry out his threat. She also wondered if she should call his bluff.

But she continued to get ready, finally deciding to wear her still damp hair pulled back into a neat chignon. Then, taking a deep breath to steady her nerves, she opened the door to face him once again.

He had resumed his perusal of the magazine but

glanced up at her. "Very nice, except for the hair. I prefer it down."

"Too bad. It stays up," she said with an angry toss of her golden head. She turned to busy herself throwing some things into a small bag. But when she heard the chair creak as he stood, she whirled about quickly.

The smile on his face was remarkably free of sarcasm. "You have only yourself to blame, you know."

"What are you talking about? I haven't encouraged you . . ."

Still smiling he shook his head. "No, you certainly haven't done that. But that icy formality just goads me into saying and doing things I shouldn't."

"You had no right to assume that I would want to have dinner with you, Alex."

He nodded. "True enough. But you knew how to reach me if it didn't suit you."

Amanda nodded slightly, acknowledging the truth of that statement. But she was still not mollified. "You still had no reason to embarrass me in front of Peter like that."

It was his turn to nod in agreement. "You're right, but as I said, your sense of outraged propriety drove me to that. Will you accept my apology, or would you like me to explain to Peter?"

Amanda turned away from those piercing slate gray eyes. "No, that won't be necessary. I'm ready to leave now."

He made some attempts at conversation enroute to the airport, but she answered in monosyllables. She was still angry with him, apology or not. And she had begun to wonder about the conditions of his financial backing of the film. Amanda came from a long line of men trained in law, and she could not believe that Peter would not have gotten some kind of firm financial commitment before undertaking the project. She would have to find out.

She felt slightly better. Alex Wojyclas would find out that she was not some naive little actress who could be threatened like this.

When they arrived at the landing strip, she was surprised to find it deserted. To her question about the pilot, he answered that he had decided to take the opportunity to get in some flying time. He helped her into the small blue and white Cessna, and she tingled strangely at the touch of those calloused fingers. As she stole a glance at him while he checked the controls, she realized that Alex Wojyclas had already made a powerful impression on her. She quickly decided that it was because he was so different from the men she was accustomed to.

They took off into the dusty blue sky, and she watched the largely empty land slide away beneath them. It was not her first time in a small plane, but she didn't exactly feel comfortable about it either. But then she didn't feel comfortable about anything at the moment.

Instead of using the crowded Dallas–Fort Worth Airport, they landed at a smaller field outside the city. A limousine awaited them. When they arrived at their destination—a very elegant downtown restaurant—Alex got out quickly while the driver assisted Amanda.

"Take Miss Adams' bag back to the hotel and be back for us in an hour and a half." Alex issued clipped orders to the driver.

Amanda wondered if he ever said "please." Somehow she doubted it. Curtness was something she disliked intensely and she added it to the list of complaints she had against the man.

Once inside the restaurant, Alex was greeted warmly by the maitre d', who seemed to know him, and they were quickly led to their table. But before they could reach it, they were stopped by a huge bear of a man who almost dwarfed even Alex, if not by height, certainly by his breadth. He boomed a greeting to Alex while eying Amanda appreciatively.

Alex returned the greeting with surprising warmth and dropped an arm casually about Amanda's waist. Even though the gesture was vaguely proprietorial, Amanda could not bring herself to resist him.

"Amanda, this is Billy Joe Hartnett." Turning to the man he said, "Billy Joe, I doubt if I need to introduce Amanda to you."

"No indeed, you don't. It's a real pleasure, ma'am. I hope you're enjoying your stay in Texas." There was a friendly quality to the man, and Amanda found herself warming up to him.

"It's nice to meet you, Mr. Hartnett. And yes, I'm enjoying my stay, although I don't get to see much more than empty range land most of the time." She smiled at him.

"Well, in that case, little lady, tell this man of yours to bring you out for a weekend at my place, and I'll show you what a working ranch is like. The kids would be in seventh heaven to have a movie star on the place."

Amanda cringed inwardly at his reference to "this man of yours," but before she could make a suitable reply, Alex cut in smoothly.

"An excellent idea, Billy Joe. We'll plan on it. I'll be in touch."

The other man gave them a cheery good-bye, and they proceeded to their table.

The interlude had served to lighten the mood. After they had ordered drinks, Alex said "Billy Joe is an authentic Texan. You should see that place of his. Swimming pool, tennis courts, golf course. And cattle grazing among the oil derricks. Some working ranch." He laughed, shaking his head in wonder. Then he gave her a serious look and asked, "Would you like to go?"

Amanda raised her eyebrows in teasing surprise. "Are you actually asking me?"

"As a matter of fact, I am. Billy Joe is a good friend, and I wouldn't take you there if I thought you would be rude." He paused, giving her a speculative look. "But you wouldn't do that, would you? Your sense of propriety would never permit you to be rude to them, even if you were angry with me." Mockery was clearly written across the rugged features.

She was about to reply when the waiter arrived with their drinks. As soon as he had departed with their dinner orders, she resumed the conversation.

"Do you find my upbringing amusing, Alex?" There was a defiant lift to her chin.

He leaned back in his chair and regarded her with

an unfathomable expression. "Perhaps I do. But it suits you very well, Amanda. The prim and proper sex goddess. You must admit it is a bit unusual." The lines around his strong mouth were mocking.

She shot him an angry look. "I'm sure I must be very different from all the other women you know." A picture of the fiery Laura Shannon came unbidden to her mind.

His reply was decidedly nonchalant. "I suppose you are, although I've had plenty of time to meet quite a variety, you know."

"Then why do you bother with one who has given you no indication that she seeks your company?" Although aware of the rudeness of her question, she still could not resist asking it.

He reached across the table and stilled her hand that toyed nervously with the decorative swizzle stick. "Because I don't know any others at the moment who intrigue me as much as you do, Amanda. And I think you are here with me because you feel the same way about me."

Reluctant to meet his eyes she stared at the large hand that covered hers so completely. He was right, but she would never admit to him that he intrgued her.

When she finally did look up into his disconcertingly direct gaze, she said haughtily, "I'm sure you could find intriguing women elsewhere."

"No doubt I could" was his noncommittal response.

During the rest of the dinner, it seemed as though they were both intent upon avoiding personal conversation. Amanda had to admit that he could be very good company. He had a quick intelligence and a wide-ranging knowledge and was, as she had noted before, a very good listener.

Back at the hotel, she felt very conspicuous waiting with him at the desk while he picked up a key and paused to scan several messages.

They were walking toward the elevators when a chilling thought suddenly struck Amanda. Alex had picked up only one key. Surely he couldn't mean that . . . Even in her mind she left the sentence unfinished. She jumped when his hand lightly touched her urging her into the elevator.

She numbly followed him down the red and white hallway, the numbness quickly replaced by anger as he inserted the key into a lock. Later, she was very glad that he had not seen the look of relief on her face when she realized that it was a suite. Doors stood open on either side of the comfortable sitting room, and she could see her bag in one of them.

When she hesitated, he turned to her. "Would you like some sherry, or perhaps brandy?"

"Sherry will be fine, thanks," she said, knowing that she should excuse herself to study the script for the next day's shooting.

However, it was almost an hour before she finally stood up and announced she really had to go over the script. She said good night, thanked him for dinner, and turned to go to her room.

But he too had stood up. He quickly caught her arm and spun her about to face him. She stared straight ahead for a moment, at the lapel of his jacket. Then he gently cupped her chin in his hands and pulled her face up to meet his gaze.

"Surely, even in your circles a good-night kiss is permissible after the second date."

The protest she was trying to form died quickly as his mouth descended, while he continued to hold her face imprisoned in his rough grasp. His other arm circled her waist drawing her to him.

There was no subtlety to his mastery of her senses. He simply took what she gave unprotestingly. His firm male lips moved sensuously over her softer ones, teasing, arousing a need as yet undefined. A tongue flicked almost casually against her own, forcing a response. Her full breasts, flattened against his hard chest, experienced a sudden tingling awareness. Then she was suddenly released. She swayed slightly as she was deprived of his muscular support.

He laughed softly. "So the sex goddess has never even been properly kissed?"

She saw the amusement dancing in his eyes, but she was too confused by her own reaction to be angry with him. Without giving any thought to what she was doing, she put a hand to her kiss-swollen lips and stared blankly at him.

Gently taking her hand away he kissed her lightly this time, his lips barely brushing against hers.

"Go to bed, Amanda. There aren't enough hours in this night to correct your sadly neglected education. That will have to wait."

She fled to her room, his words ringing in her ears.

"Peter, I just cannot believe this." The look on Amanda's face was one of undisguised shock. "How could you undertake a film without being certain of the money?"

Peter threw her a surprised look. "Amanda, it's the way it's done. The money men always reserve the right to withdraw financing if they choose. Of course, it means that they lose money so it doesn't happen very often. But some of them make real pests of themselves, always wanting this or that changed." He rolled his dark eyes heavenward. "Thank heaven I've got one this time who seems content to stay out of it."

But Amanda wasn't so certain about that. She sat in Peter's room lost in thought until he finally broke the silence.

"Anyway, why are you so interested in this? I had the impression that the financial arrangements weren't of any interest to you."

Amanda forced herself away from her mental wanderings. For a moment, she was tempted to tell Peter that Alex had made just such a threat. But what was to be gained by it? First of all, she doubted that he would actually carry out his threat. And secondly, she was reluctant to involve Peter in a matter over which he could have no control.

But Peter's question required an answer. "I was just curious, that's all. Alex mentioned something that led me to believe that his financial commitment was limited."

Peter looked at her shrewdly. "Amanda, are you having problems with him?"

She colored slightly but shook her head firmly. "Nothing I can't handle, Peter." Then she quickly changed the subject.

4

Amanda recalled Alex's description of the Hartnett ranch as she rode up the long, tree-lined drive, with the effusive Billy Joe chattering nonstop.

She had been surprised when Billy Joe's wife, Lu, had contacted her at the motel to invite her for the weekend. She wanted to refuse, but Lu had seemed so warm and friendly, and she did want to get away for a weekend. Although Alex's name had not even been mentioned, Amanda assumed that he would be there and had mixed feelings about it. However, when Billy Joe met her at the airport alone she realized that she was disappointed not to find Alex there.

But her disappointment was short-lived. After greeting her warmly Billy Joe told her that Alex would be flying in directly to the ranch. She was bemused to find that she really did want to see him.

She had been relaxing beside the large pool for

about an hour when she heard the drone of a small plane overhead. Shielding her eyes from the glare of the Texas sun, she looked up just as Lu's voice beside her proclaimed her thoughts.

"That must be Alex. He never misses an opportunity to fly out here himself. I'll never understand what men see in flying around in those tiny things. They just don't seem safe to me."

Amanda laughed and agreed with her.

A short time later she heard male voices approaching, and Alex and Billy Joe appeared on the terrace. Lu had gotten up at their approach and stretched to give Alex a friendly kiss.

Amanda also rose from her chaise lounge and felt her pulse quickening at the sight of Alex clad in a light gray business suit that emphasized his dark, rugged good looks.

His eyes made a slow inspection of her scantily clad form before he bent to kiss her lightly. Even the light pressure of his mouth on hers sent a tingling warmth through her, and made Amanda wonder just how she did feel about him.

He excused himself and reappeared a short time later in brief black trunks. As he executed a clean knife dive into the turquoise water, she openly gaped at the superbly fit and powerful body she could only guess at before. There was no denying that she found him attractive.

Moments later he swam over to the side nearest her and splashed some water in her direction. "Aren't you going to join me?"

She nodded and went over to the edge. "I'll get in

at the shallow end. I'm really not a strong swimmer, and I don't like jumping into water over my head."

But he held out his arms. "Come on. I'll catch you."

She would have refused, except that Billy Joe had come up to them. "Go ahead, Amanda. I'll make sure he behaves himself," he teased.

And so with great reluctance she jumped in, a small cry escaping from her as the cold water struck her. Alex's strong arms held her securely, and she flung her own arms about his neck until she got used to the water.

A splash behind them told her that Billy Joe, too, had jumped in, and the shock waves from his considerable bulk hitting the water threw her more closely against Alex.

"I must remember to thank Billy Joe for that," Alex murmured as he held her to him.

She made a move to smooth her long hair from her face, but he did it for her, then rubbed a thumb lightly across her moist lips. His mouth had just begun a slow descent when they were interrupted by shouts from the Hartnett children who had just arrived at the pool.

"Damn," he swore softly, before turning his attention to the children, who seemed excited to see him.

After a brief swim Amanda clambered out of the pool, which had been taken over by the Hartnett children, Alex and Billy Joe for a game of water basketball. She resumed her seat and watched them with amusement. It occurred to her that she was now seeing yet another side of that complex man as she watched him gambol unabashedly with the others.

"I can see I'll have to do something or the children

will take him over for the weekend, just as they always do." Lu had come up to stand near her while watching the action in the pool.

Amanda glanced up at her with a smile. "I was just thinking how different he seems here."

Lu laughed. "When Alex first came here he was so stiff and formal that I wanted to shake him. But I think he's gotten used to our ways by now. Life hasn't always been easy for him, you know."

Amanda recalled Alex's statement at her parents' home that his father had been an immigrant miner. But surely it hadn't been all that bad. After all, mines had been unionized long ago, and while she knew it was dirty, dangerous work, she was under the assumption that miners were fairly well paid. She wanted to ask Lu what she meant but, reluctant to betray her ignorance about Alex's background, she kept her silence.

That evening Amanda was tuning her guitar and paying little attention to the babble of voices around her. It had been a pleasant day, and she was very glad she had come. She truly liked the Hartnett family. But their warmth and exuberance served as a nagging reminder of how different they were from her own family. Even Alex seemed different, as though he too had been caught up in the atmosphere of the ranch.

When she finally completed her tuning and looked up at the waiting circle of admirers, she gazed directly into Alex's gray eyes. Then she forced herself to become aware of the others. Lu and Billy Joe had invited several neighbors in for a barbecue, and the children had each been permitted to invite a friend.

There was quite a group gathered in the huge "rumpus room," as Billy Joe called it. Amanda had done very little singing lately and was glad for the opportunity.

Quickly she launched into the most popular song from her album. The children squealed with delight, and were quickly silenced by the adults. After a few more songs, Amanda asked if there were any requests —and of course there were. So she sang some more. Then to her surprise Alex asked her to sing the theme song from her first film. Amanda hadn't sung the song since recording it for the sound track, but she did her best and the expression on his face confirmed that he was pleased.

Much later Alex asked her to go for a stroll with him before retiring. Amanda was lulled into a sense of comfort in his presence by this time. He seemed such a different man.

"I was surprised at your request. I haven't done that song since I recorded it for the sound track." She was curious and looked up at him for an answer.

He glanced down at her as they walked slowly along the golf course that partially surrounded the big house. "I was at a party at Jack Destler's some time ago, and he treated us to a partial screening of your film. I was bored and ready to leave until I heard you singing that song."

Amanda was silent. She disliked being reminded of Alex's involvement with the Hollywood social set and most especially Laura Shannon. Had he been there with her that night?

They were walking side by side without touching.

Then he reached out to grasp her hand lightly, engulfing it totally. Although she had begun to feel a certain familiarity with his touch, it was still an unwelcome reminder of the uniqueness of this man. However, she made no effort to remove her hand, and they continued their walk along a tree-lined fairway, coming at last to a white-fenced paddock where Billy Joe kept his prize bull. She paused and glanced over the moonlit scene. The bull was nowhere in sight at the moment.

The silence weighed heavily on them, and in an effort to dispel its presence Amanda told him how much she had enjoyed the weekend. He made no response, but cupped a hand about each bare shoulder and drew her gently to him. It crossed her mind fleetingly that there was no way she would ever mistake his touch for any other man's. She made no effort to resist but felt a trembling begin deep inside.

His hand lifted her chin. His mouth closed warmly over hers, gentle at first, moving with sensual slowness against the softness of her parted lips. Her hands crept of their own volition up to encircle his neck and entwine themselves in the thickly curling dark hair above his collar.

Quickly he gathered her more tightly to him, until she was being supported wholly by his hard male frame. The kiss became more demanding as his tongue flicked into her mouth, sending strange new sensations through her body as it was caressed and molded ever closer to him.

Amanda was not thinking—just feeling—and the feeling was pleasant. So, when the fear struck, it struck doubly hard this time because it was not anticipated. One of his hands had strayed to cup a full breast, and she then became aware of what was happening.

She stiffened and pushed against him, straining hard. He let her go, and she stepped back quickly putting several feet between them. Having done so, she could not speak. It was as though his kisses had paralyzed her lips.

When she finally looked up at him, she saw a slightly puzzled look on his dark features. "Still trying to decide, Amanda?" His voice sounded harsh in the gentle stillness of the night.

It was her turn to look puzzled. "Wh . . . what do you mean?"

"Whether it's the sex goddess or the socialite." There was no mistaking the mockery in his voice. All gentleness and fear vanished in the sudden surge of anger.

"Alex, I don't find your characterizations amusing."

"No?" He raised one dark brow. "When you do reach a decision, let me know. If it's the right one, I just might be interested."

He inclined his head to her very slightly, then turned on his heel and started back to the house. She stared after him for a moment and then followed—but at a distance.

Amanda told herself that it was an invitation she simply could not refuse. Alex had offered her the opportunity to spend a weekend at home. It was her grandmother's birthday, and Amanda had longed to be home for the celebration. Without Alex's intervention she would not have been able to do so, and she was grateful to him. Still she had strangely mixed feelings about seeing him again.

Alex had called her at the end of a long and difficult day. For this reason, she was less guarded than she might have been and told him of her desire to be home for the birthday celebration. When he offered to arrange for her to be off and to accompany him back to New York in the company jet, she had eagerly seized the opportunity.

After they had made the necessary arrangements and said good-bye, she leaned back tiredly and thought about him. The weekend with the Hartnetts had started very pleasantly but had ended under a cloud.

Amanda had gone off to bed upset and confused after their stroll. She was confused by her response to his kiss. In truth, she knew that she was very inexperienced where men were concerned—and she certainly had no experience with men like Alex. But she was too honest to deny that he certainly had a devastating effect on her senses.

She wondered if her fear of his caresses was the result of the incident of so many years ago or a subconscious reminder that Alex was a collector of actresses. Certainly his parting remark to her that night gave her ample reason to know his true intentions where she was concerned. The next day he continued to be pleasant enough to her, but she could sense that it was all for the benefit of their host and hostess.

Amanda was relieved when she boarded the big jet for the trip to New York to find that they would not be alone. Five men and a woman were already aboard. Alex was nowhere to be seen. He had sent a small plane to pick her up at the landing strip after convincing Peter to let her off for a few days. They were filming six days a week now, and she felt guilty about leaving. There were numerous scenes that could be shot without her, however, including a difficult one with her stunt woman stand-in.

After the others had introduced themselves, she settled down into one of the comfortable seats. A steward had brought her a glass of wine from a bar located at the rear of the cabin. She decided that she was certainly flying home in luxury. The big jet had about thirty seats, all arranged in small groups with tables between them. At the front of the cabin were two desks for more serious work. Occasional aromas drifting up from the rear of the cabin suggested that there was also an excellent galley. This was confirmed when the steward inquired whether she would prefer *coq au vin* or roast beef for dinner.

He had just departed when Alex appeared accompanied by several other men. Amanda was once again struck by the incongruity of the perfectly tailored tan suit he wore and the essential roughness he portrayed. His disinterested gaze swept over the group, pausing only when it found her. She felt an unwelcome fluttering as their eyes locked momentarily. He took the empty seat in the group where she sat, his rather formal greeting to her at odds with the smoldering charcoal look he gave her.

The roar of the great engines on take-off prevented any conversation for a few moments, and then the pilot announced that they could remove their belts. The steward promptly brought Alex a drink—obviously he knew his boss's preferences. Talk then resumed about them.

"You've lost weight, Amanda." He made a deliberately slow sweep of her, pausing for too long a moment where the first button of her silk shirt barely concealed the rising swell of her breasts.

Her hand fluttered nervously to fasten another button. "I . . . we have all been working very hard. I feel guilty about leaving when the others will all be working."

He shrugged unconcernedly. "They're all veterans. It won't bother them."

"Just when does one attain the status of veteran, I wonder?" There was a slight edge to her tone, since he seemed to be once again referring to her as a dilettante.

He threw her an amused look. "In your case, probably never."

Amanda gave him an icy glare in return, and he promptly got up and joined another group in what was apparently a business discussion. Amanda was left to converse with the other woman aboard who asked questions about film making and expressed a great interest in Dack Temple.

They landed at Kennedy Airport right on schedule. Alex had arranged for a limousine to drive her over to La Guardia, where she could catch the Eastern

shuttle flight to Boston. He had not spoken to her
again except to say good-bye and wish her a pleasant
weekend at home.

Her response that she hoped his would be pleasant
too brought a smile to the rugged features.

"I intend it to be."

Amanda felt that she could not have misinterpreted
his meaning, and found herself wondering how he
kept them all straight. Perhaps he didn't even bother
trying.

Her flight to Boston was uneventful, and her brother awaited her at Logan Airport. It was good to be
home.

The party for her grandmother was held in the
afternoon in deference to that venerable lady's early
bedtime. Amanda had just returned home when she
was called to the phone. She assumed that it was Jay
calling to see what time he should pick her up for
dinner, but the voice on the other end was not Jay's.

"Amanda? It's Alex. I'm glad I reached you. In case
you haven't heard, there is a traffic controllers' strike
scheduled for midnight tonight at Logan. Since we
must get back to Dallas tomorrow evening, I would
suggest that you get yourself down here tonight."

Amanda hadn't heard the news. She had been
looking forward to the evening with Jay and was
disappointed that she would have to return early.

"When is your grandmother's party?"

She broke her silence to respond to his question.
"I've just returned from it."

"Good. Then you won't have to miss it. You could
try to book from another airport or drive to New York

70

tomorrow, but I would suggest that you come down tonight."

Amanda thought about it. It would be difficult, with the strike, to book from another airport, and there were really no other large airports in the area. She did not relish the prospects of driving to New York the next day either. She decided to call Jay, plan an early dinner, and still be on the way to New York before the midnight deadline.

To Alex she said, "Yes, you're right. I will come down this evening."

"Good. I'll have someone meet you at the airport. You're welcome to stay here tonight," he added matter-of-factly.

Without giving much thought to it, Amanda accepted. He told her he was giving a dinner party which would undoubtedly still be in progress when she arrived.

She then reached Jay and they planned an early dinner. He was disappointed, of course, but then so was she.

When Jay arrived, he quickly gathered her into his arms and kissed her gently. Amanda could not avoid the comparisons that sprang so readily to her mind. Kissing Jay felt safe and familiar. Two years ago he had asked her to marry him. She had refused, of course, but he had let her know that the offer still stood. And she knew that he meant it. There were even times when she believed she might one day accept his proposal. It was always part of a hazily perceived future, however, and her rational mind told her that future would really never arrive.

But still she watched him as they enjoyed their dinner in the same restaurant Alex had taken her months earlier. She wondered why she could not love Jay. Being with him seemed, in some ways, so right. Even though it was completely unnecessary, from Amanda's point of view, her family was constantly reminding her of that fact. Only Sam refrained from nagging her about Jay—no doubt because of his long-standing friendship with the man whom she regarded as another brother.

Two hours later she was being met at La Guardia by the chauffeur Alex had sent. As the car glided noiselessly across the grand old 59th Street Bridge into Manhattan, Amanda began to think nervously of the consequences of her acceptance of Alex's hospitality. She knew that she should have insisted upon staying at a hotel. But it had seemed at the time to be rude to refuse his invitation. Now she wondered if the risk of being thought rude might not have been preferable to staying overnight in the same apartment with him.

Alex met her as she stepped off the elevator, and she relived that first meeting. She had to admit that he still unnerved her just as he had done the other time. It was not a comforting thought. Fortunately for her peace of mind the dinner party was still going on. There were about a dozen people present, and Alex saw that she was introduced around. Most of the women present were in long gowns, and Amanda felt somewhat out of place in an off-white silk shirtwaist that she had worn to dinner.

She was rather surprised to find that none of the guests present appeared to have any connection with the film world. They were all corporate and Wall Street people—except for one woman whom Amanda immediately recognized. Stacey Laing was one of a handful of top models whose names were known to the public. Amanda seemed to recall reading somewhere that she had just signed for her first film. She was taller than Amanda by at least four inches and had an enviable mane of long honey blond hair.

It did not take much guessing on Amanda's part to ascertain that she was Alex's date. Much as the voluptuous Laura Shannon had done before her, Stacey clung to Alex at every possible opportunity. Obviously, thought Amanda, he likes that type of woman. And Amanda was not at all fooled by Stacey's too bright smile. Amanda, too, had spent enough time posing for photographers to know how one can perfect that smile—so natural in appearance, but completely artificial in fact. Stacy seemed to regard her as a rival of sorts.

Amanda spent the remainder of the party aware of Stacey's icy glares and the occasional unreadable looks of her host. It was not the most comfortable situation she had ever been in, and she wished again that she had gone to a hotel. She didn't know whether to be relieved or apprehensive as the guests began to depart. Stacey was the last to leave, after giving Amanda one last, distinctly unfriendly look. Alex followed her out into the hall for a moment, apparently to say good night in private.

By the time he returned, Amanda was busy gathering up glasses, cups and ash trays. Saying nothing, he crossed the room to a comfortable chair, sat down, and picked up the brandy snifter he had apparently left there earlier. She was picking up some glasses from a nearby table when a long arm shot out suddenly, grasping hers.

"Leave it, Amanda. My housekeeper will be here early in the morning to clean up the mess." It was a velvet-clothed order.

Amanda set down the glasses and straightened up to face him. His hand slid down to grasp her own small hand. "Come here, Amanda." His tone was the same as before, but this time she did not obey.

Before she could do more than utter a small gasp of surprise, he moved quickly to scoop her into his arms and settle her on his lap.

The lingering traces of the cigar he had smoked earlier and the now familiar scent of tangy cologne assaulted her senses, already overwhelmed at the closeness of him. The solidly muscled thighs beneath her and the steel band that circled her and held her fast gave her an unwelcome sense of helplessness. She sat rigidly, staring down at her hands which were folded nervously in her lap.

"Honey, will you relax?" There was an exasperated edge to his voice.

"Please let me go, Alex." The sound of her own calm and cool voice surprised her.

"No, I will not let you go. I rather like you where you are." Then, with a deep chuckle, he added, "Of course, I can think of a place where I would rather have you."

She drew herself up haughtily. "As a substitute for Stacey Laing?"

But, whatever reaction she had expected to her unkind remark, it was not what she got. He said nothing, simply wrapped a rough hand around her face and drew her gently to him. For a moment she resisted, holding herself stiffly apart from the mouth poised tantalizingly near her own. Amanda could already feel the imprint of his lips on hers, and she quickly yielded them to him. It was a softly persuasive kiss, and to her surprise he was the one who ended it.

"You're still a virgin, aren't you, Amanda?" Those gray eyes, darker now in the dim light, searched hers deeply for a moment and then continued. "It's not something that ever mattered much to me before. But I want to be the first for you." He drew a calloused thumb very slowly across her slightly parted lips, then rested a curved hand against her neck.

"Why?" Her voice was husky.

For a moment his eyes remained on her full lips, before he raised them to meet her wide-eyed stare.

"Why? Because you intrigue me. I told you that before. Because somewhere beneath that very proper exterior there just might be a passionate core. And I intend to be the one to find it."

"No," she gasped in response as he grasped the pale shining hair that flowed down her back and crushed it against her head, pulling her to him.

His hard male mouth hovered for just a fraction of a second, barely touching her kiss-softened lips. And then he claimed them slowly, teasing them with easy mastery. A persuasive tongue forced its way into her mouth, sending a curling sensation through her slim form that was being molded to his unyielding male contours. Slowly, expertly, he explored the resisting softness of her tongue, probing sensuously.

All the while his hands were caressing her heated skin. The clinging silk fabric of her dress offered her little protection from the intimate roamings of his hands, hands that took possession of her body as easily as his mouth had exerted its unquestioned domination of hers.

One hand cupped a full breast, the thumb rubbing lightly against a suddenly unbearably sensitive nipple. The covering silk seemed to melt away. Alex reluctantly moved away from her mouth and trailed light kisses across her cheek to a delicate earlobe.

"Mandy, Mandy, let me have you." His voice was a groaning whisper, and his warm breath fanned against the ultrasensitive cord along the side of her neck.

She responded with a soft moan as she arched her neck to allow him easier access to this new territory. Lost in new sensations she paid scant attention to the hand that was busy undoing the buttons of her dress.

His hand slipped quickly inside the dress, impatiently pushing the silky bra aside and gently fondling the softness that lay exposed.

His crisp black hair brushed lightly against her face as he lowered his head to explore the new territory uncovered by roving hands. His tongue rolled lightly across the swelling fullness until it reached the rosy tip, teasing it to button hardness. Amanda was weak, breathless and totally lost in strange, new sensations.

The hand that had cupped her breast now sought new conquests, moving down across her lap to her leg and sliding up slowly along the inside of her thigh.

Somehow the warning bell that had been clamoring unheeded in the recesses of her bedazzled mind broke through to her consciousness, and she reacted explosively.

"No." The strength of her voice shocked her. She gripped his forearm with amazing strength and dragged his hand away. He then raised his head and looked at her. For a moment she felt the force of his desire and almost gave in to it.

But he leaned back then, resting his head against the back of the chair as he loosened his grip on her very slightly. "Amanda, I'm not one of your well brought up young gentlemen. I'm a man with a man's needs. And I intend to turn you into a woman— tonight or later. I can afford to be patient because I know you want me."

The last was said with such authority that she could not refute it. And considering the way she had responded to him, it would have been ludicrous to try. So she tried instead to make him understand the fears she thought had been deeply buried.

"Alex, you don't understand. I . . ." She faltered, knowing that she could not explain adequately.

He shook his head angrily. "They really did a number on you, didn't they?" Seeing her sharp glance he went on. "Brought up to be a perfect lady but not to be a woman."

Realizing what he meant Amanda became angry. "I suppose it would have been better if I had been brought up like some . . . some tramp from the street."

He laughed at that. "I just can't imagine that

somehow. But no, I simply meant that if you had been allowed to be exposed to the usual experiences somewhere along the way it might have been different."

"I assume you mean like all your other women." She was now sitting stiffly in his lap, her blue eyes blazing at him.

His expression did not change, except that his eyes danced with silver lights. "But you aren't one of 'my women' yet."

She jumped up suddenly, catching him by surprise. When she had put some distance between them, she turned on him, hands planted firmly on rounded hips. "And I won't be, either. I will never be part of your string, Alex."

His derisive laughter followed her as she fled from the room. Her heart pounded wildly as she considered just how close she had come to being just that.

"Cut, damn it. Tyler, you're coming on too strong. Didn't they ever teach you subtlety?" Peter's voice took on an irritated tone, something they heard only infrequently.

Amanda felt absolutely no sympathy for the man. Jared Tyler had succeeded in alienating all of them at one time or another. Even the normally even-tempered Dack Temple had exploded at him just yesterday, using to his face the nickname they had all privately used for some time: "Jar-head." He was arrogant, argumentative and sometimes downright vicious.

Playing this scene with him taxed Amanda's acting

skills to the limits. His role as Dack's nephew, with whom Amanda had an affair, made it necessary for her to work long and intimately with him, and this scene, where Jared first declares his intentions toward his new "aunt," was especially difficult. The scene was already in its third retake and Amanda's patience was wearing thin.

Peter called a short break and they all headed gratefully to the refreshment van that had accompanied them. It was a warm day and the humidity was on the rise. Amanda took a glass of lemonade and started across to the makeup man, who was beckoning her imperiously. This weather wreaked havoc on both makeup and hair and she saw the hair stylist moving toward her, too.

The last stray wisp of pale blond hair had been coaxed back into place and the necessary repairs to her makeup completed just as she saw Peter moving purposefully toward the cameras once more. She started to get up from the folding chair, but then sank back again as she saw that Peter had been distracted by the arrival of a Jeep.

"Bless him, whoever he is," muttered Margaret Melville, an older character actress who played Amanda's housekeeper. She too had been summoned over for some necessary repairs and had settled her ample figure into a chair next to Amanda's

Amanda turned idly to see who was arriving in a cloud of dust. When the driver unfolded his long frame from the little Jeep, she gasped in amazement. It was Alex.

"Well, if it isn't our dark 'angel.' He's certainly

picked the wrong time to come to see how his film is progressing." The older actress chuckled.

Amanda nodded in agreement, but felt herself beginning to panic. This scene was going to be difficult enough without his presence. Still, he had every right and reason to be here—even if he picked the worst possible time.

She watched with rapt attention as Peter went over to greet him and felt once more that terrifying vulnerability as he turned to glance in her direction. The two men talked for a few minutes and then they were all called to the set once more.

As she walked over to the old barn that formed a backdrop for the scene Amanda was conscious of Alex's eyes on her. She avoided them for as long as she could, but finally forced herself to face him. He was standing beside Peter, dwarfing the smaller director with his impressive bulk. Dressed casually in khaki slacks and a deep-red knit shirt, he looked very much at ease. She reminded herself sternly that this was her world—not his—and she wasn't about to let him turn it upside down.

But a few minutes later she knew that he had done just that. First she forgot her place and had to be reminded by the set manager. In the next fifteen minutes she stumbled over her lines, played to the wrong camera and tripped over a roll of fence wire that she knew perfectly well was where it belonged. Since Alex was standing with Peter she couldn't avoid seeing him every time Peter interrupted with a curt "cut." Finally the director came over and drew her aside.

"Amanda, what's wrong? Are you feeling okay?" Peter's voice was concerned and Amanda felt compelled to tell him the truth. It would have been so much easier to go along with the excuse Peter was offering.

"It's Alex. He makes me nervous. Why is he here?" She risked a quick glance at him and found him watching her with a slight frown.

"He was in the area and just decided to fly out to see how things are going. He's entitled to that, you know—although I could wish he had chosen a better time. Look, Mandy, I don't know what's going on between you two, but I can't very well order him off the set and we're behind schedule already." Peter was almost pleading with her and Amanda felt guilty.

She squared her shoulders. "I'm sorry, Peter. This hasn't been a good day for any of us, I guess. I'll be all right now."

And somehow she was. They shot the scene once more and finally Peter triumphantly called it a "wrap." Amanda almost sank to the ground in relief. Then, ignoring Alex completely, she went off to her trailer-cum-dressing room to rid herself of the makeup and cumbersome long dress.

When she emerged, she found Alex waiting for her. There was no avoiding him this time. The others were all at work dismantling the equipment or heading toward the Jeeps that would carry them back to the motel.

"Are you all right, Amanda?" His dark eyes raked over her.

She nodded, avoiding his gaze. "I'm just tired. It's been a difficult day."

"Let me drive you back. A shower and a cool drink should help." He took her arm and led her toward the Jeep he had driven out to the set.

She wanted to refuse, but she was touched by his seemingly genuine concern and went along, very conscious of his arm curved possessively about her waist.

Once they were on the road Amanda settled back in her seat and closed her eyes as she tried not to think about the man beside her. Being with him at this moment did somehow seem right to her. But it was a very fragile sense of "rightness," capable of being shattered by one wrong word from either of them.

Before long they were pulling in to the little motel and Amanda turned to him. "Are you staying here tonight, Alex?"

Once again those dark eyes rested on her as he pulled to a stop near her door. "I had planned to see if you would like to fly to Dallas for dinner, but you look too tired for that. What do you usually do for dinner here?"

Amanda grimaced. "I ignore it as much as possible."

He laughed briefly, then took in her slim form with a look that missed nothing. "I thought as much. You're losing weight."

"I know," she replied as she allowed him to help her from the Jeep. "The food here isn't really that bad, but I don't seem to have much appetite after a day like this."

She fumbled with her key and he took it from her and opened the door. The blessed coolness of the room brought a sigh of relief from her and she almost forgot him until she heard the door closing behind her.

He came up behind her and gripped her shoulders lightly, kneading the taut muscles. "Why don't you go relax in a warm tub and I'll see what I can do about dinner?"

She relaxed against his hard frame and felt his lips brush lightly against the top of her head. And then he was gone.

Amanda drew an almost full tub of warm water, threw in a generous amount of her favorite bath salts and submerged herself gratefully in the fragrant warmth. After she had scrubbed away the day's dust and sweat she pillowed her head against a rolled up towel and leaned back tiredly.

"Have you fallen asleep in there?" A voice and the accompanying tap on the door aroused her. For a moment she was confused. Alex? She shook her head to rid herself of the cobwebs.

"Mandy, answer me." She heard the anxiety in his voice, then saw the doorknob turn. He opened the door and she saw concern turn quickly to relief and then to desire as he saw her there. She returned his stare mutely.

"I'm sorry if I startled you, but I knocked several times. Were you asleep?" He continued to stand in the doorway.

She nodded, hugging her knees to her chest in a not-too-successful attempt to cover herself. He looked briefly at the large bath towel that she had left on the vanity and she followed his gaze—and his thoughts. But before she could say or do anything he backed out of the room.

A few minutes later she emerged dressed in an Indian caftan, her long, still-wet hair combed and tucked behind her ears. She discovered that she was indeed hungry as the smell of food teased her. She burst into laughter.

"This is a poor substitute for dinner in Dallas, but right now it looks better than a steak to me." She reached for a bag of French fries and nibbled on one before checking out the rest of the meal. "A giant burger and a chocolate shake. Who could ask for anything more?" She laughed as she unwrapped the rest of her dinner and seated herself cross-legged on the bed.

He took the over-stuffed chair across from her, and they ate in silence for a while. Then he gave her a considering look.

"Do you really see yourself making a career out of this?"

For a moment she was reminded of the earlier remarks he had made about her lack of seriousness, but she dismissed the thought. She didn't want to destroy the uneasy camaraderie that had sprung up between them. "Yes, but I think I'll try to be more selective about locations in the future."

He chuckled at that and returned to his dinner. When they had both finished he gathered up the remains and disposed of them while she sank back against the pillows with a contented sigh.

Even when he came back to her and sat down on

the edge of the bed she couldn't feel any alarm. It must be the exhaustion.

He leaned over her, watching her reaction closely. "You're not afraid of me right now, are you?" He reached out to stroke her cheek lightly. "If you weren't so tired . . ." His voice trailed off as he slowly lowered his head.

Even the images evoked by his words failed to stir her. She made a feeble attempt to raise her arms to hold him, but finally let them fall back as his lips brushed lightly against hers.

The last thing she remembered was the gentleness of his kiss.

5

~~~~~~~~~~~~~~~~

Amanda stretched her lithe form and readjusted the pillows on the bed. The days in Texas were dwindling down to a final busy few, and the hectic pace was taking its toll on her. She was trying to concentrate on the script, but her thoughts persisted in straying back to that night in New York three weeks ago.

Amanda now saw that night for what it was—a watershed in her life. It had taken her many days and much thought before she would admit to herself that she wanted him as she had never wanted any other man. Alex, damn him, had been right. She was tormented by his knowledge of her desire for him.

She had tried excuse after excuse to explain the hold he had over her—his vast experience as opposed to her own inexperience; the very uniqueness of the man; his naturally dominating manner. But none of the reasons could account for it in her mind. She always returned to the very first time she had seen him. That strange chemistry that operated on a frighteningly primitive level had been there even then. To someone brought up as Amanda had been, there was a faintly repugnant air to such feelings. Nevertheless, these feelings were very real.

Yet there was another explanation. The word hovered about in her mind even though she refused to consider it seriously. Love. Was it possible? She did not think so. There were things about Alex she did not even really like. Although she had to admit that even those qualities were an inescapable part of the man she was so attracted to.

After she had undressed and gotten into bed, she drifted off into an uneasy sleep wondering if she would have an affair with him. Or had her behavior finally driven him off? She suspected that he thought of her as a tease and did not know how to tell him the true nature of her fears. How could she, when she wasn't even sure herself? She was smiling to herself as she fell asleep thinking about the unlikely prospect of calling him and saying, "Alex, I would like to have an affair with you."

However, the opportunity presented itself a few days later. The day's filming had been tiresome. Amanda's presence had been required for a total of not more than an hour. But, because that time was split between several scenes, she had been forced to remain at the set all day.

It had been a sultry day. The temperature remained high, but the aridity was gone. There was a heaviness to the air that they had not felt before. Far to the south the tropical depressions that could turn into full-fledged hurricanes were beginning to be reported. It was only a matter of time before one of them reached official hurricane status and began churning up the weather as it wandered about the Gulf of Mexico. They were racing against time now, and everyone was tense.

So Amanda was exhausted, more from lack of activity than from hard work, when she returned to the motel. After showering and shampooing her hair, she had dropped wearily onto the bed, deciding to take a short nap before dinner. In fact she wasn't certain that she wanted dinner at all. The nearby restaurant had long since lost its homey attraction to them. It seemed that the owner-cook had a very limited repertory, and they had exhausted it long ago. The only alternatives were pizza or Mexican food. The latter had resulted in severe gastrointestinal problems for Amanda and several other members of the crew. She was losing weight as it was, and the wardrobe staff complained constantly about it.

She had drifted off into a light sleep when the phone rang. Her confused mind thought at first it was a wake-up call. But then she recognized the deep voice.

"Alex?" she murmured sleepily.

"Amanda, are you all right? Your voice sounds strange."

Did he actually sound concerned? As she shook herself awake, she was surprised. "I . . . I'm all right, Alex. I was just sleeping, that's all."

"At seven o'clock? It sounds to me as though this career of yours has finally gotten to you."

Amanda bristled slightly at the sneer she imagined on his face. "It was a particularly tiring day," she replied rather stiffly.

"How soon will you be finished there?"

Amanda sighed. "Another three or four days if all goes well."

"The weather may hurry you a bit. We lost two men on a drilling rig in the Gulf today. The hurricane season is beginning."

Amanda frowned, thinking that his voice showed none of the concern that should have been there even though he obviously wouldn't have known them personally. But, she decided bitterly, his tone would have been the same if he had. The man probably had no emotions.

"Yes, that's why we're working so hard."

"You have a three-week break after this, don't you?"

So he knew their schedule. She merely affirmed that she did but began to grow slightly nervous. Thinking about having an affair with him and actually making the necessary plans were two different matters entirely. She was already rethinking her decision.

Uncomfortable with the silence on the line, she said that she intended to go home to relax and enjoy a New England fall.

"Would you consider coming to Wyoming for a few days to enjoy a Wyoming fall?" There was a softly seductive quality to his voice.

There it was—the opportunity she wanted and feared. She stalled for time. "Y . . . you grew up there, didn't you?"

"Yes, and I have a home there. I plan to take some time off myself, and I thought you might want to join me."

She thought that a strange thing for him to say since she had shown little inclination to seek his company to date. But that thought was put aside for the moment while she considered the implications of her decision. If she said yes, they would be spending more time together than they had up to this time, and the thought of having an affair with him would no doubt become a reality. On the other hand, if she said no she guessed that he would accept that as an end to their relationship. And she suddenly knew that she did not want it to end.

Taking a deep breath to steady herself, she said "Yes" in a barely audible tone. She had a sharp sense of having sealed her own doom with that word.

"Good." Did he actually sound relieved? "I'll make the arrangements. Now go back to sleep, honey. You sound as though you need it."

After they had hung up, Amanda sat in bed staring at the phone that had provided the temporary link between them. She wondered if he too had sensed that this call marked either the end of their relationship or the beginning of their affair. She knew that Alex wanted her, but he was far too attractive a man to continue to chase one reluctant blonde when there were many others to be had for the taking. And so he might well have decided, before making that call, that he would make one last attempt and then turn his attentions elsewhere. It was not a comforting thought. One little "no," and he would have been out of her life forever. But she had not been able to say that word.

Amanda was suddenly filled with self-loathing. She had told him she would never become one of his women, and yet she had all but agreed to do just that. Why was she prepared to have an affair with a man she didn't love, and to whom marriage was out of the question even if she did love him?

Amanda felt that Alex would marry one day but only to have an heir. Marriage would never confine him. He just wasn't monogamous. That was patently obvious.

She spent the remaining days of filming alternating between thoughts of calling him to cancel the plans and nervously anticipating those plans. Each evening, when she returned to the motel, her eyes would inevitably be drawn to the phone. But she did nothing.

When she returned from the next to the last day's filming, she had a message from him with instructions about when she would be picked up, and so on. She wondered if, had she talked to him, instead of just receiving the message, she would have backed out.

Amanda returned early from the party they had at the nearby restaurant to celebrate the end of location filming. She was too exhausted from hard work and lack of sleep to party that night. She had just returned to her room when the phone rang. It was Sam. As soon as she heard his voice, she felt a sudden pang of guilt. She had completely forgotten to tell her family that she would not be coming home directly. Of course, they had not been told exactly when the filming would be completed, so they couldn't be expecting her at any particular time. But they did know of the forthcoming break.

"How's it going, golden girl?" Sam's easy use of the pet name brought out a strong desire to reach back to that less complicated past.

"We finished today, Sam, and not a moment too soon for me. I think I'll never get Texas dust out of me."

"Then you'll be home tomorrow?"

Amanda tensed, knowing what was to come. "No, Sam. I'll be home in about a week. I'm going to Wyoming for a few days with Alex Wojyclas." She had almost not added that last phrase. But she knew no one else in Wyoming, and Sam would know that.

There was a long silence, and Amanda bit her lip nervously. "Mandy, do you know what you're doing?" Sam's voice was careful, almost as though he thought she might have taken leave of her senses.

She sighed heavily. "Yes, Sam. I know what I'm doing." She knew that her voice sounded far more certain than she felt at the moment.

"Mandy, you know that I've always stood by you, even when Mother and Dad felt you were making the wrong choices. But I just don't understand—"

She cut in quickly, not wanting to hear the rest. "Sam, please. I'm a big girl now, and I can choose my own friends."

She heard a disgusted snort from Sam. "Somehow,

I doubt that friendship is what he has in mind, Amanda."

She was really upset now. Sam never called her by her full name unless he was angry about something. But her reply was even enough. "You may be right, Sam. But I can handle it, even so."

It seemed that Sam recognized the note of finality in her voice, and they hung up after she had given him the telephone number in Wyoming that Alex had given her. Nothing was said about what he would tell her parents, but she knew that it would not be the truth.

The call had shaken her more than she cared to admit. She sensed a loosening of the ties to her family and a drawing away from Sam, brother and best friend.

True to his word Alex had made all the arrangements. Amanda found that it was very easy to allow him to take charge of her life, just as it had always been easy to allow her family to do it in the past. While it was true that she had rebelled in some rather spectacular ways, she had always retained the impression that they had been in charge of her life. Had she ever truly been her own person?

As she settled into her seat in the small plane and buckled her belt in accordance with the pilot's instructions, she thought about the extent of her family's influence on her.

While Amanda had rebelled in some ways against her parents, it had always been made much easier by

Sam's encouragement. However, she had always remained within that select circle of "old families" where her friendships had been concerned. The few times that she had ventured outside that lofty group had not gone well.

At Yale she had remained, for the most part, within a group of students very much like herself. She had occasionally taken home a friend drawn from outside the charmed circle, but her parents' pained expressions and strained formality had either driven them away or caused her to give them up. It had never been a conscious decision—it had just happened.

She recalled the time her grandmother had somehow learned that Amanda was dating the son of a prominent Irish politician in Boston. They had met at Yale where he was attending law school, and she had seen him over school holidays at home. His family had been in Boston for over a hundred years and were respectable business people. Nevertheless, Elizabeth Lowell had fixed her still brilliant blue eyes unwaveringly on her favorite granddaughter and said quite distinctly that he "simply isn't one of us." Amanda had not dated him again even though she had liked him.

She wondered what her grandmother would think about Alex Wojyclas. The answer to that was too unpleasant to consider. That brought to her mind again the fact that she knew nothing about Alex's family. She was actually quite curious. Perhaps she would get to meet them if they still lived in Wyoming.

A few moments later they landed at the same small airport in suburban Dallas that Alex had used before. The pilot helped her from the plane and retrieved her luggage from the seat behind them. There were numerous small aircraft on the apron and one very elegant looking plane—a swan among a flock of ducks. The pilot indicated that plane. "This way, Miss Adams."

At that moment two men appeared on the tarmac from an ugly building she assumed was the terminal. They too approached the plane and stopped, waiting for Amanda and the pilot.

They exchanged greetings, introduced themselves, and inquired whether or not she wanted something to eat, saying that there were sandwiches on board. Amanda stated that sandwiches were fine and turned to the plane admiringly. "What a beautiful plane. What is it?"

"It's a Learjet, Miss Adams. Let me assure you that it is as beautiful to fly as it is to look at. We'll be in Jackson in about three hours."

Amanda was impressed. She had heard of Learjets but had never actually seen one that she could recall. When she boarded she was even more surprised. It was very small inside. The graceful exterior had given the impression of much more space. Although she could stand upright, the two pilots had to stoop over within the confines of the plane, and the seats were close to the floor. But it was luxuriously appointed with a tiny kitchenette in one corner.

The take-off was truly wondrous. The plane seemed to soar straight up. There was none of the gradual lifting into the heavens that she had experienced in other small planes. She was quite fascinated.

After they had levelled off and one of the pilots told

her she could remove her seat belt, she explored the contents of the small refrigerator located just behind the cockpit. Before getting herself something to drink, she went forward to inquire if either of the men wanted anything. The pilot declined, but the younger copilot asked for some soda.

When she brought it to him, he gave her a grin and, turning to his companion, said, "Just wait till I tell the folks back home that we had Amanda Adams playing stewardess on this trip."

Amanda joined in the laughter and lingered for a while, crouching behind the two men and asking numerous questions about the plane and the bewildering array of instruments. She learned that this too was owned by CRI and would soon be sold to make way for a new plane—a Learfan that was much more fuel efficient. As the two men began what promised to be a lengthy discussion of the new plane, she excused herself and resumed her seat.

Her hands toyed nervously with her drink. Amanda did not ordinarily drink hard liquor, but she had fixed herself a rather strong gin and tonic—much too early in the day, she thought—and on an empty stomach at that. She had had breakfast, but that had been six hours ago. She put aside the drink and went back to the refrigerator. There were several wrapped sandwiches and some brie. She selected a roast beef sandwich and took it back to her seat where she forced herself to eat all of it.

She wondered for the thousandth time if she could really go through with this. The thought propelled her once more to the bar to replenish her drink. Perhaps she should get drunk. She never had, of course, but she had heard that alcohol would lessen one's inhibitions. A friend in California had confided to her that she had once been so drunk that she couldn't even remember what she had done. But the thought was not appealing. Amanda disliked losing control of herself. Resolutely she put aside the half-finished drink and settled back in the comfortable seat. She had slept poorly the previous night, and she was tired.

She was startled into wakefulness by a hand lightly touching her shoulder and opened her eyes to see the copilot standing over her. "We'll be landing in a few moments, Miss Adams."

She could hardly believe that she had slept most of the way. She straightened up and fastened her belt.

Amanda saw Alex as soon as she stepped from the plane. He was striding toward them, tall and rugged, clad in a business suit, but with the tie gone and his shirt collar open.

Amanda shivered partly from the cool wind that blew against her and partly, she knew, from fear. For a brief moment she considered running back into the plane and demanding to be taken away from here. But that was out of the question.

"Welcome to Wyoming," he murmured as he dropped a light kiss on her upturned face.

"I didn't expect such a change in temperature," she said, shivering once again. It had been quite warm in Texas when she left and she had worn trousers and a light silk shirt.

He laughed. "It's almost winter here." Quickly, he shrugged out of his jacket and put it around her shoulders. She snuggled gratefully into its outsized warmth, still carrying a trace of his cologne and the ever-present pungent aroma of a cigar.

Alex had turned his attention to the two men briefly, and, after Amanda had thanked them and said good-bye, he led her to a blue BMW parked nearby, stowed her bags in the trunk, and helped her into the car.

Finally alone with him, her nervousness compelled her to chatter endlessly about the final days of filming. And when she had exhausted that subject, she asked him if his family still lived in Wyoming. He had been silent most of the time, except to make brief comments about some of the things she had related. She suddenly had the sense that he had hardly been listening to her.

He turned briefly now to regard her with a challenging expression. "The only family I have left is a sister, and she lives in Palo Alto."

"Oh," she said, then asked, "Is your home here the one you grew up in, then?" That seemed logical to her, since most people she knew had homes that had been in their families for generations.

A long silence followed and she saw the muscle along his firm jaw tense abruptly. He had returned his attention to the road, and, for a moment, she thought that he was not going to answer.

"No." His answer was brief and to the point and seemed not to invite further questions.

Knowing that he was upset for some reason, she turned away from him and gazed out the window. She had expected autumn foliage, but there was very little. Most of the trees that grew up the sides of the steep

hills were evergreens. In the distance were the magnificent Tetons, wearing their caps of snow. It was wild
and primitive country. The highway they had been
traveling was nearly deserted, and Alex was driving
fast. Suddenly he slowed down and, after seeming to
hesitate for a second, turned off onto a narrow road in
a poor state of repair. Amanda was about to ask him
how far they had to go, but when she turned back to
him his expression stopped her.

Seen only in profile, there was a rigid set to his
strong jaw. Her attention was jolted away as he turned
once again, this time onto a dirt road that was deeply
rutted and dusty.

In a few minutes they crested a small hill and began
to descend slowly into a narrow valley. It was a
desolate scene. She turned questioningly to him just as
he came to a stop. Before she could say anything, he
had gotten out of the car, striding quickly around to
her side and opening the door. He reached in and she
automatically gave him her hand, but she could not
imagine what they were doing here.

Spread before them were a group of tumbledown
shacks, all obviously deserted. Some had apparently
fallen down of their own accord, while others had
been reduced to a pile of unsightly rubble by a large
yellow bulldozer that squatted in their midst. It was a
slightly eerie and thoroughly depressing scene.

"This is where I grew up, Amanda." His booming
voice startled her in the strange silence about them.
But it was a voice devoid of any emotion.

Her eyes opened wide as she stared dumbly from
him to the ugly scene. He was not looking at her. He

gestured to one of the piles of rubble. "That was my home. Three rooms. I shared a bedroom with my sister and my brother. We were better off than a lot of others."

He started to walk toward a slightly larger building without bothering to see if she were following. For a moment she just stood rooted in place, then quickly started to follow his long strides. As she reached him he stopped in front of a building which she suddenly recognized as a one-room schoolhouse. She had seen them in rural New England, where many were either lovingly preserved or converted into charming homes. But this one was ugly and dilapidated. Little remained of the white paint that had covered it.

Alex was testing the two steps that led to the open doorway. When he was certain that they would hold his weight, he turned and extended a hand to her. She silently gave it to him and followed him inside.

Several broken desks were piled in one corner, and a cracked blackboard ran the length of the front of the room. All else was dust and rubble. "This was where I went to school for the first eight years. This was a mining camp. In those days the government didn't pay much attention to small mines like this, and the unions hadn't gotten around to organizing here. My father, like most of the others, was an immigrant miner. He worked twelve-hour shifts, six days a week.

"Most of the boys quit school after the eighth grade and went into the mines. My brother was one of them. He was six years older than I was, and he had weak lungs. I used to lie awake at night and listen to him cough. He died before his twenty-fifth birthday.

"That would probably have been my fate too if it hadn't been for football. The teacher kept telling my parents that I should continue my schooling, but we needed the money. Sometimes, I used to play football with my friends after school, out there in the school-yard. My teacher's brother was coach at the regional high school, and he was the one who finally talked my parents into letting me continue.

"So I travelled thirty miles each day to the high school, played football, and worked in the mines after school and on weekends the rest of the year.

"During my senior year, the coach arranged to have a scout come from Stanford to see me play and I was given a scholarship. The rest I've told you. Dad died here the day I went to New York to accept the Heisman Trophy. I had sold my extra tickets to the Rose Bowl to pay their way, but he was already too sick to make the trip. The mines had finally gotten him.

"Mother died not long after, and, when I went off to Palo Alto, my sister Kate came with me and worked as a waitress to support herself while she finished school at night. She eventually went to college too and taught school until she married and had a family."

All this was told in tones devoid of any emotion. He might have been reciting from a textbook. Amanda felt a chill that was not caused by the wind blowing through the broken windows. She could not imagine what it must have been like. Her mind refused to consider it and she could therefore think of nothing to say.

He then led her back outside and they walked in

silence to the car. "Has that satisfied your curiosity, Amanda?" His gray eyes were like steel slivers piercing through her. He reached for the car door.

She refused to look up at him and swallowed to loosen the lump in her throat. He opened the door and she slid quickly onto the leather seat.

They were all the way back to the main road before she could trust her voice. "Do you hate me for the privileges I've had, Alex?" Her voice sounded shaky and small as she forced herself to look at him.

He didn't turn to face her, but she saw him shake his head slowly. "No. That you grew up as you did was no more your doing than it was mine that I grew up back there."

She leaned back against the headrest, her head aching from her thoughts. She was certain that he did hate her for the privileged life she had led. She recalled the evening of their first dinner date in Boston, when she had had a sudden impression that he actually disliked her. Now she knew she had not been wrong.

Most of all she regretted that she had ever learned all this. It was cowardly, she knew, but it would have been so much better if she had never known. She shivered as she thought about the ruthless determination this man must have had to have survived in such an environment. If Alex had seemed different to her before, that difference now looked gargantuan in her mind. A great chasm had opened between them, and she knew it could never be crossed.

Coming here had been a terrible mistake, and she ached with a longing for the familiarity of her home.

6

We're here."

Amanda jumped, startled by the sound of his voice. Neither of them had spoken for more than half an hour. Without really seeing anything, she had been staring out the side window and now she focused her eyes on their surroundings.

He was ascending a steep driveway lined with rows of stately pines and hemlocks. At the top was a small clearing and in the midst of the clearing sat the house. It was a rambling modern masterpiece, sprawling over the uneven ground in the manner of very modern homes. Built entirely of wood and stone, it blended well with its surroundings. She had just a brief glimpse of it before he pressed the automatic garage door opener and the car slid quietly into the dim recess of the garage.

His withdrawal from her seemed to persist as he gathered their luggage from the trunk and led the way into the house. Her comments about the house drew only monosyllabic responses, and so she fell silent, feeling terribly uncomfortable.

When he deposited her bags in a small but attractively furnished bedroom, she realized with a start that the matter of sleeping arrangements, which had earlier been such a concern to her, had vanished altogether from her mind.

"I'll leave you to unpack and change into something warmer," he said as she removed his jacket from her shoulders and handed it to him. "I would rather not go out to dinner tonight. It's a long drive into town, and there's nothing much there, in any event. Will a steak be all right with you?"

Amanda absently nodded her agreement and turned without a word to unpack. She assumed that he had left the room, but he was still there when she turned to carry some clothes to the closet. Their eyes met briefly. Then he turned and quickly left the room.

Though she had lingered a long time with her unpacking and changing, she still did not know what to say to him when she finally found her way back to the kitchen to confront him. She found him mixing a marinade for the steak.

"Can you actually cook?" She stared at him in surprise, forgetting for the moment the things she knew she should say.

His gray gaze swept dispassionately over her jeans-and-sweater-clad figure and then returned to the marinade. "I learned to cook because I like to eat. I discovered a long time ago that I don't like having servants around any more than necessary. So learning to cook was simply the lesser of two evils, as far as I'm concerned." His voice was clipped, indicating that his mood had not changed.

In a desperate attempt to lighten the atmosphere Amanda laughed. "Well, I'll be glad to relieve you of the burden beginning tomorrow morning, when I've had a chance to learn where things are. I haven't had much opportunity to cook lately."

Without glancing at her, he said, "I'm surprised that you can cook at all. You certainly must have had a cook all your life."

It became rapidly apparent to Amanda that she could do nothing to change his mood, and as a result her own patience was wearing thin. She folded her arms across her chest in a gesture of disgust. "As a matter of fact, Alex, we never had a cook. My mother did all the cooking and had help only for large dinner parties."

Her tone brought his attention quickly to her. "Dinner parties?" he said mockingly. "In my home dinner parties consisted of sharing the available food with less fortunate neighbors."

She wanted to slap him. He was deliberately goading her. "Alex, is this what I can expect for the next few days? Constant reminders of my privileged upbringing?" Her voice had risen in anger.

He put down the spoon he had been using to stir the marinade and turned to stare at her, his expression grim. But before he could say anything, Amanda turned sharply on her heels and left the kitchen.

When he later joined her in the downstairs family room, she had fixed herself a drink—rather stronger than she liked. Amanda felt the need of some fortification if she were to get through this evening with him.

He said nothing while he poured himself a generous drink. The silence lay heavily upon them, filling the air with a tension that was almost palpable. Finally, he asked her if she would like to sit out on the deck for a while before it became too cool. She nodded her assent, assuming that the deck in question lay behind the closed drapes on one wall of the room. But he had started back up the stairs, finally pausing and turning to her.

"This way—the deck is off the master bedroom." He led her up yet another small set of stairs near her room. She hesitated in the doorway, then gasped in delight. It was a lovely room done in pale beige and warm browns. A huge platform bed dominated one side of the room. In the opposite corner the floor dropped to a semicircular area before a stone fireplace. Brightly colored pillows were scattered about the rim, where the floor dropped off. A shiver ran through her as she stared at the opulent sensuality of the scene.

She was still standing transfixed in the doorway when he walked across the room and pulled open the drapes to reveal glass doors leading to a wooden deck.

She followed him through the door and stopped once again. The deck was cantilevered over the edge of a steep cliff. The view was truly breathtaking— forests of evergreens marching off to purple-hued mountains whose caps of snow were turning softly pink in the glow of the lowering sun.

"Oh, this is magnificent." She walked over to the edge of the deck and breathed in deeply, her eyes feasting on the scene.

"Are you glad you've come here, Amanda?" His voice came from just beside her ear. She had been so enthralled by the view that she had not heard him come up behind her.

She nodded and then risked a sidelong glance at him. There had been no mockery in his voice, and she could only hope that his unpleasant mood had passed.

He circled her with his long arms, and she leaned back against him, that strange longing beginning inside her as her body registered the touch of his hard male form. After a few moments he dropped his arms and moved away to one of the green canvas-covered chaise lounges nearby. She followed him, reluctantly turning away from the view.

"Why did you come?"

Amanda took a sip from her drink, wondering if she should be honest and tell him that she didn't really know. After all, she had been asking herself that question ever since she had agreed to come here.

"I don't know." The words slipped out because they were the only words she seemed to know at the moment. She looked at him to see his reaction.

To her astonishment, he laughed. "Somehow, I think that's an honest answer." Then his eyes grew dark and serious as he went on. "Amanda, I'm sorry if what I showed you back there shocked you." He stopped, then suddenly got up and began to pace about the small deck, one hand rubbing the back of his neck thoughtfully.

"No, that's not true. I'm not sorry. You needed to see that. Maybe you should have seen it as it was when I lived there. Have you ever truly seen poverty, Amanda?" He turned on her suddenly.

She gestured helplessly. "I . . . I used to do some volunteer work at a children's center in South Boston." She expected him to make some sarcastic remark and braced herself for it. But it did not come.

"I showed you that place for a reason, you know. I wanted you to see for yourself what the differences are between us." He kept his gaze levelled on her as he spoke.

His honesty and lack of sarcasm gave her courage and she responded truthfully. "I've always been aware of the differences between us, Alex. I may not have known the reason behind them, but I haven't been blind."

"I'm glad to hear that." He moved toward the doorway. "Come along. You can fix the salad while I grill the steak."

She followed him silently back into the house wondering why he had thought it necessary to point out to her the differences between them. Was he warning her somehow?

The conversation was carefully impersonal during dinner. Afterward he asked her to clean up while he made some business calls. He returned to the kitchen just as she was finishing and suggested they have coffee before the fire he had just built.

She thought—hoped—that he was referring to the fireplace in the family room, but he led the way back to the master bedroom. Amanda's stomach was churning. The setting was too intimate.

They settled themselves before the crackling fire, several feet between them. The tension had returned, stronger than ever. She finally looked at him over the rim of her upraised mug of coffee. "Are you sorry you invited me, Alex?"

He looked at her for a long time in silence, causing her to squirm uncomfortably under his scrutiny. "No, I'm not sorry. But I had expected you to say no."

"I almost did." Her words were barely audible over the crackling blaze in the fireplace.

"Which brings us back to the reason you agreed."

She made no answer to that and pretended to concentrate on her coffee.

"Especially in view of the fact that I've made my intentions pretty plain." She felt her face begin to flush hotly, knowing that he was watching her.

Out of the corner of her eye, she saw him move toward her, and her heart began to pound unmercifully. With very little effort, he forced her back against the cushions as he held her face in both his hands. His kiss was gentle, undemanding, and she responded by wrapping her arms about his neck. Finally, he moved away from her mouth to explore her neck. A slow, reluctant fire was spreading through her, gathering strength with every flick of his roving tongue.

She felt him begin to undo the buttons of her sweater and made a small sound of protest. But her token attempts to push away his hands met with no success, and she knew that he could sense that she was not really resisting. She gasped softly as he brushed aside the soft fabric and slid a hand inside to caress her heated skin. He had returned his attention to her soft lips, and that probing tongue began a sensuous exploration of her mouth. She was scarcely aware of his hands at her back undoing the clasp of her bra.

When he held her away from him for a moment to free her of both sweater and bra, she began to tremble. "Alex, please." A part of her wanted this—but another part was denying that desire.

He remained slightly apart from her and quickly pulled off his own light sweater. They remained that way for a long moment, suspended in time, separated by several feet. She could not take her eyes from him—the solidly muscled chest with its mat of dark, curling hair, and the desire-filled eyes that devoured her naked smoothness.

Involuntarily she reached out to him, and that one small movement was all that was necessary. He pulled her to him. The sudden contact with that hard chest sent shock waves through her. He held her like that for a long time, stroking the fine golden hair that flowed down her bare back. She could feel his heart thudding noisily in his chest—or was it her own?

At length he lay her back against the cushions, touching her only with his eyes. Then his dark head descended, and his firm male lips claimed a soft breast, quickly teasing the rosy tip into a stiffened awareness. He repeated his actions with the other one, and she arched toward him, purring sounds coming from her mouth as tremors suffused her slim body.

By the time he reluctantly returned to claim her mouth once more, Amanda felt herself drowning in a whirlpool of ecstasy. It seemed that her flesh had been made for him alone to caress and possess.

But even so, when he began to tug at the zipper of her jeans, the fear returned—the sensation stronger, perhaps because his expert mastery of her senses had heightened all feeling.

"No. I . . . I can't." She pushed him away. For a moment they sat there facing each other, fear in her deep blue eyes, and dark, fathomless desire in his smoldering charcoal gaze.

She struggled to her feet and turned to flee the room. But he got up quickly and caught her around the waist. The hairs on his forearms tickled lightly against the soft undersides of her full breasts, reminding her of the pleasure of his touch.

"Please let me go, Alex. I want to go to bed."

"You're sleeping here, with me, Amanda." His tone was firm as his breath fanned against the top of her head.

"No." She ceased her struggles, knowing them to be useless.

"Yes, little one. Go get ready for bed. But if you're not back here quickly, I'll come get you." He released her, and she ran headlong out the door, almost stumbling down the few steps to her own room.

Once in the relative safety of her room, she forced herself to go about the routine of a lifetime—

undressing, washing her face, and finally sitting down at the small vanity to brush the tangles from her long hair. Her hands trembled, and she could see the uneven rise and fall of her chest above the low neckline of her nightgown.

She was still brushing her hair when she heard the sound of the door being opened. His reflection joined hers in the mirror.

"Alex, please, I want to sleep here." She looked at his reflection rather than the man himself. He took the brush from her hand, and ran his hand through the long hair that still crackled from its fierce brushing.

"If that was what you really wanted, Amanda, you could have locked the door." He smiled down at her, but it was a gentle smile free of the cynicism his words might have implied.

It was true. She knew that there was a lock on the door but hadn't used it. She tilted her head back to look up at him, and his lips brushed lightly against her smooth brow. In the next instant, she was swept into his arms and carried off to his room.

He dropped her gently onto the big bed. She turned away as he began to undress, but when he climbed in beside her, she rolled over onto her back to find him raised above her, watching her with more tenderness than she would have thought possible on those rugged features. The fires that had begun to burn earlier were being rekindled.

"Sleep, honey. I won't touch you until you're ready." His lips barely touched hers before he dropped down beside her and cradled her against him.

She wanted to say that she was ready, but the words would not come out. So she lay there, thinking that she would never be able to sleep. She felt very protected yet terribly vulnerable. When sleep finally overtook her, she was thinking that in the morning she would try to explain her fears to him.

She awoke to find sunlight streaming through a narrow crack in the heavy draperies and the other half of the bed empty. For a few moments she actually wondered if she had only imagined that he had been there. It was ridiculous of course. She knew that as she was roused to complete wakefulness. How else could she have gotten into his bed?

She rolled over onto her side and stared at the empty pillow that still bore the imprint of his head. Did she wish that he were still there? If he had been, would she have been able to explain her fears to him or would explanations have been unnecessary?

For a long time Amanda lay quietly in the big bed, thinking. Was her fear really a reaction to that horror of seven years ago? Or was she only seizing upon that as an excuse to avoid becoming involved with a man whose nature was as yet unknown to her? Amanda had always prided herself on her ability to judge people accurately, but this man remained an engima to her. Was he the cynical playboy he sometimes seemed to be? Or was the tender, gentle man in whose arms she had fallen asleep last night the real Alex? There was no way of telling.

Finally, she got out of bed and drew open the heavy brown drapes to reveal a magnificent day. She slid open the glass doors and stepped barefoot onto the deck. The morning air was quite chill, and she hugged herself, shivering, as she breathed in the crispness.

"If you're planning to catch pneumonia, I'd like you to know that the nearest hospital is about fifty miles away." She whirled about to find him standing there, leaning casually against the door frame, an amused expression on the rugged features. She was suddenly aware of the flimsiness of her gown for more reasons. than the cold air and hurried back into the warmth of the room, feeling once again that strange electricity that seemed to flow between them every time she was near him.

"It was silly of me. But it was so beautiful that I just couldn't resist." She smiled up at him as she rubbed her bare arms.

He opened a closet door and took out a deep wine-colored velour robe which he held open for her. She snuggled gratefully into its warmth, feeling much like a small child trying on adult clothes as she rolled up the too-long sleeves.

He slowly drew her around to face him and tilted up her chin to receive a slow, gentle kiss. "Did you sleep well?"

"Yes," she murmured huskily as he teased the corners of her mouth with small kisses.

When he released her, she wanted to cling to him, hold him to her. Instead, she fussed unnecessarily with the tie of the robe.

"Would you like to go riding this afternoon?"

"Oh yes," she breathed. "It's a perfect day for it."

"Fine. I have a conference call at noon, but we can go after that."

She frowned. "A conference call? I thought you were on vacation."

He gave her a rueful smile. "Unfortunately, honey, in my position one can never truly be on vacation. But this is as close as I've come to it for a long time."

Amanda was vaguely irritated when his call seemed to be lasting an extraordinarily long time. She had dressed in worn jeans and boots and a dusty rose wool sweater and was ready to leave long before he had finished his call.

But when he appeared on the small terrace off the family room where she had been pacing restlessly, she quickly forgot her anger. He seemed very real to her now, dressed in a blue plaid wool shirt and jeans that showed as much wear as her own. This is how she always pictured him in her mind—the rugged outdoorsman, not the well-tailored corporate executive.

She couldn't suppress a smile which drew a quizzical raising of his dark brows. "You look now the way I've always pictured you," she explained, the smile lingering on her softly tinted lips.

"I can't very well go riding in a business suit," he said with what was obviously an attempt at lightness. But she sensed that she had upset him somehow.

As they were driving to a nearby ranch, Amanda stole a quick glance at him, wondering why he had taken offense at her casual remark. She wished that she could ask him but was unable to do so. It brought back that unwelcome thought she had had when she awoke this morning—that she really didn't know him very well.

But he seemed to have shrugged off whatever had bothered him as he explained to her that the ranch where they would be riding belonged to an old friend. He had called him earlier, and they were invited to visit for a while after their ride. Amanda was looking forward to that. It would be interesting to meet people who had known Alex for a long time. Would it provide an insight into this tantalizingly complex man?

"Alex, you wouldn't . . . kill anything?" Amanda stared in undisguised horror as Alex took down a well-polished rifle from a rack in the small tack room.

He threw her an amused look. "No, Mandy. Not unless it tries to kill us first."

He laughed aloud at her wide-eyed look.

"Honey, these are not your tame New England woods. There are cougars and bears out there and even an occasional pack of wolves. But we're not likely to see anything. Don't worry."

She had promptly felt guilty about her too-quick assumption that he intended to harm some poor little creature. And it brought to her once again how little she knew of him. She followed him at a leisurely pace away from the ranch headquarters. Although the warmth of the sun had banished the chill from the air, there was a stiff breeze that kept her from being too warm in her woolen sweater. She was riding a well-behaved bay gelding, who nonetheless showed his eagerness to run.

Alex was several lengths ahead on a magnificent gray stallion—a tall powerful creature that came close to dwarfing Alex's impressive stature. He rode with deceptive ease, completely in control of the fractious animal without giving the slightest appearance of exerting any control. The range land quickly gave way to small pine-covered hills, and they crossed a sparkling little stream, pausing to allow the horses to drink, then drinking themselves.

As she tried to put her mouth to the water, holding back her long hair with one hand, she almost tumbled in. Even before a frightened squeal escaped completely from her lips, he had grabbed her. As she bent to drink, he held her long hair away for her, the back of his hand rubbing pleasurably against her neck.

Then he pulled her to her feet and pressed her to his long length. As he held her that way for a long moment, she was startled by a sudden awareness of the two of them and this particular moment in time. She could not have said why, but she knew that this was one of those moments that would remain forever etched into her mind.

The warmth of the sun, the deep blue of the sky, the babbling of the little stream as it scampered over mossy rocks, and the scents of horses, pine and leather—all were committed forever to her mind. But most of all she would remember him as he stood before her—tall and powerful even in this primitive land. He belonged here while she belonged to the rocky soil of New England. And the two worlds seemed so far apart.

By the time they returned to the ranch headquarters, Amanda was beginning to suspect that she would pay dearly for these hours in the saddle. She had not ridden for so long in a number of years and was already aware of abused muscles that would be protesting tomorrow.

They turned over their mounts to one of the ranch hands and walked over to the big white frame ranch house.

Both their host and hostess came to greet them. Patty and Dave Logan were an attractive couple. They both greeted Alex with unrestrained warmth, a warmth which he returned in kind. Amanda was pleasantly surprised at their natural friendliness toward her. As she became a major star, she had found, to her dismay, that people tended to treat her differently when they met her. But such stiffness was missing here, and she was very grateful for its absence.

The four of them sat in the big, comfortable living room for a while, drinking coffee and enjoying some of Patty's freshly baked brownies. The men had entered into a discussion of breeding stock, and Dave stood up, followed quickly by Alex. He announced that they were going out to the barns for a while.

Amanda was not at all displeased about this. It had become apparent from the conversation that both Dave and Patty had known Alex since childhood and Amanda hoped that with Alex and Dave gone she could elicit some information from Patty. She wasn't exactly sure just what she was seeking, perhaps some elusive key that would unlock his secrets to her. It was worth a try.

As soon as the men had departed, Patty curled comfortably into her chair and grinned at Amanda. "Well, Alex certainly surprised us this time. I nearly

118

flipped when Dave told me he had brought someone with him."

Amanda frowned at the elfin redhead who sat across from her. At first, she had assumed that Patty's surprise stemmed from who she was, but her last words seemed to disprove that.

"Do you mean that he usually comes here alone?"

Patty nodded. "Always. I've kidded him about it, and he always said he came here to get away from women as well as work."

Amanda disgested that. In spite of herself, she felt quite pleased. She had imagined that she was merely the latest in a long line of women he had brought to this rural retreat. Her attention was then drawn back to Patty who had gone on to ask Amanda about the film she was currently working on. Amanda sensed an opportunity lost. She had intended to pursue Patty's remark and elicit more information about Alex, but she was forced to talk about the film, and, of course, about Dack Temple.

Patty heaved an exaggerated sigh. "I think I've been in love with Dack Temple for at least fifteen years—along with every other woman in America. So please don't tell me he's nasty and conceited. I couldn't bear it." Her blue eyes twinkled. Amanda assured her that Dack was anything but that. In truth she liked Dack quite a lot. Dack was a legendary practical joker and she told Patty about some of the incidents that had lightened their lengthy stay in Texas.

Both women laughed at the tales, but then Patty leaned forward eagerly. "But tell me what it's like to kiss him. It must be heavenly."

She was so serious that Amanda had to stifle a smile. "Kissing someone on a movie set with several cameras trained on you and dozens of people watching is not exactly intimate, Patty."

Patty was clearly disappointed, but Amanda's thoughts were not on kissing Dack at all. She was thinking of the only man who could produce the kind of reaction Patty was obviously thinking of.

"When I saw Dack and Alex together, I couldn't help thinking that Alex is clearly the more attractive of the two." She was recalling the night of Alex's party. How long ago it seemed.

Patty sipped her coffee thoughtfully. "I suppose you're right. But I've known Alex for so long, you know, that I just can't think of him that way."

Amanda felt her pulse rate leap. It had worked. Now perhaps she could get somewhere. "You've known Alex since you were children?"

Patty nodded, passing the brownies to Amanda, who declined. "Not really, but close, I guess. Let's see. I would have been twelve when I first met Alex. He was seventeen. I've never told him, but I had my first real crush on Alex Wojyclas."

When Patty paused, Amanda decided to push for some information. "It must have been very difficult for him, being so poor, I mean." She added that Alex had shown her where he had grown up.

Patty looked surprised. "He showed you that? I wonder why. Not that Alex has ever tried to deny his background, but still . . ." Her voice trailed off, but, just when Amanda was trying to think of a way to rephrase her question, she continued:

"It was hard for him. He was really the only one of the 'shantytowners'—that's what we used to call them. It seems awful now, but we were only kids, you know. Anyway, he was the only one accepted by the other kids. Alex was always special. Partly it was football, but mostly it was just him. He was even voted 'Most Likely to Succeed.' A wise choice for a group of kids, don't you think?"

Amanda nodded, hoping that Patty would continue. And she did, obviously warming to the subject. "But you're right. It was really tough for him. He had the most awful manners, and he couldn't afford decent clothes. But he learned fast. If he hadn't been so darned big, I'm sure he would have had to take a lot from the other boys, since all the girls were after him. You know how boys can be.

"He dated my older sister Peggy for a while. I met him when she brought him home for dinner one time. My mother was horrified at his lack of manners, but Daddy said Alex had something—that he would go far. I was fascinated by him myself."

Patty got up to refill their coffee mugs then, and Amanda was left alone for a moment with her thoughts. Having attended private schools, she had never really considered that aspect before. The children all came from backgrounds similar to her own, and she had little experience with less fortunate children. But she could recall the few scholarship students her school had taken. They were ghetto kids from the teeming slums of South Boston, and she and her friends had stayed well away from them. Although she had never poked fun at them, she could think of a number of her classmates who had. Guilt washed over her as she thought about it.

Even though Patty had said that the other kids had been afraid to tease him to his face, she knew that Alex must have sensed their secret amusement and condescension. In a sense, Amanda was sorry she had learned this. The impossibility of their relationship weighed heavily on her mind. She was sure he could never overcome the deep resentment he must have toward those like herself—born into privileged social standing with an almost instinctive knowledge of social graces.

7

~~~~~~~~~~~~~

Alex and Dave returned shortly thereafter, and she and Alex took their leave after accepting with pleasure an invitation to dinner the next evening.

Amanda was unnaturally quiet following their return to his house—so much so that Alex asked her if she were not feeling well. She considered telling him what she had learned and how she felt about it. In the end she merely said that the long ride had left her tired and slightly achy, and she announced her intention of soaking in a warm tub for a while.

Alex accepted her explanation and suggested she take her bath in the big sunken tub in the master bath, since it had a Jacuzzi which should help her aching muscles.

But she hesitated when she saw that the tub was set before a large window with no drapes. She peered out suspiciously. It was apparent that no one could see in, since that part of the house perched at the very edge of the steep cliff—and beyond was wilderness. She finally succumbed to the temptation of the Jacuzzi and slipped into the tub. As the pulsating sprays soothed her body, her mind reverted to the conversation with Patty. She really wanted to discuss it with Alex—but how?

As the evening wore on, she was no closer to finding a way of approching the subject. She had fixed dinner for them—an excellent beef ragout, one of her specialties. He had pronounced it superb, a statement she believed since there were no leftovers.

Some time after dinner, they had settled down once more before a fire in the master bedroom. Amanda could not shake the sadness that had come upon her after Patty's revelations. It was as though they were doomed before anything happened between them. She had mixed feelings at this point about having an affair with him. Her body wanted him—there was no doubting that. But her mind told her that it would be better if they remained friends.

"You've been quiet all evening, honey. Are you tired?" His deep voice cut into her thoughts.

Seizing on the proffered excuse, she nodded. "I guess I am, although I shouldn't be. I slept better last night than I have in a long time." The words were out before she could stop them. She felt herself flushing.

But it was too late. He smiled as he stood up and extended his hand to her. "Good. I suggest the same sleeping arrangements for tonight."

She gave him her hand and stood uncertainly. It was the moment of decision. If she said no, he wouldn't touch her. But if she said yes? Amanda learned at that moment that there are needs of the flesh that pay no attention at all to the dictates of the mind. She nodded her agreement.

When Amanda returned to the bedroom—of her own volition this time—he was already in bed. And the sight of his naked torso propped against the pillows triggered an ache in her that had nothing at all to do with tired muscles. She walked hesitantly to the bed, feeling very self-conscious in her pale pink nightgown. He drew back the covers for her, his eyes traveling slowly over her.

"I like you in pink. But I seem to recall having said that before." There was a teasing note in his voice that helped smooth a difficult moment for her.

"Yes, I think you did," she said, trying to match the levity of his tone.

He drew her to him and smoothed away the fine hair that always seemed to be falling across her face. The lips that claimed hers were firm but gentle in their possession and, even though his hands caressed her, he seemed to be maintaining a distance of sorts between them. Amanda responded fully to his kisses, but made no attempt to close that distance. Her mind still had some control over her wayward body after all. When they finally settled down side by side, with his arm draped casually around her, she fell asleep almost immediately, still indecisive about making the first move.

When she awoke, the first gray light of dawn was creeping into the room which smelled of the now dead fire. The first conscious thought she had was of his body beside her. She was lying on her side, and his arm lay heavily across the hollow of her waist. She could feel his other arm beneath her pillow. It seemed that each part of her body registered his touch separately, and together it added up to a very pleasant whole.

She made a small movement, and immediately heard his regular breathing change rhythm. The arm that lay across her tightened its grip slightly. And then his mouth was against her neck, pressing lightly as he murmured "good morning" in a voice still thick with sleep. She said nothing but turned to face him, knowing as she did so that there was no turning back. What was to come had been inevitable from that first meeting. She knew that now.

He gathered her tightly to him, crushing her soft breasts against his hard chest and tangling his long legs with hers. One hand pressed lightly against the small of her back, bringing her against the hardness of his desire. A fire began to consume her, catching quickly this time. There was a burning need in her loins, an ache for a fulfillment as yet unknown.

He continued to hold her, stroking a curved hip, fondling a full breast, as his lips traced fire over her face. When his face hovered scant inches above hers, she saw the question in his eyes, and he saw his answer in hers.

There was a rush of cool air across her sensitive skin as he flung back the covers to rid them both of the clothing that had suddenly become superfluous. She opened her eyes just in time to see his dark head descend to capture a rosy nipple firmly in his mouth. Flames coursed through her yearning body.

His hand trailed lightly across her stomach. When his fingers parted her, she gasped softly, arching her aching flesh to him. Forgotten were all her fears, lost forever in the flames that engulfed her as he quickly found the seat of her passion and roused her to still higher and hotter fires of need. By the time he knelt over her, she was ablaze. Nothing existed except her need for him. Their eyes met, and his unspoken question was answered by her pleading, love-glazed look.

Cupping strong hands around her bottom, he took her, gentle even in the heat of his own passion. And she knew that her body had never truly felt complete before and would never totally belong to her again. They moved in unison, giving and receiving. He murmured soft words of encouragement to her, and together they were lifted on wings of fire to dizzying heights only to soar even higher as he thrust more deeply into her. When the blinding zenith was reached, she cried out her release, and her cry mingled with his deep groan.

Afterward, he continued to hold her gently, not leaving her, stroking her still quivering body and raining soft kisses on her slowly cooling flesh. "Mandy, Mandy, how I've wanted you." He swept away the tendrils of hair that had spilled across her face, his fingers lingering feather light on her cheek as he stared down at her. "I tried to be gentle—not to hurt you. It was good for you, wasn't it?"

Suddenly embarrassed to be discussing her feelings, she buried her face in his neck and murmured a soft "yes."

"And it will get better. I promise you. The first time is never the best, honey. There's so much I want to teach you—so many ways." He lifted her face back to his, with an undemanding kiss that went on and on.

She had drifted off to sleep after their lovemaking, swept away blissfully with the lingering feeling of his hands on her, of him in her. She awoke to aching disappointment when she found him no longer there. She had wanted to awaken with him beside her and lay there for a while hoping he would return. Finally, reluctantly, she got out of bed, drew on her soft robe, and went to look for him.

As soon as she left the bedroom, she heard his voice and knew that he was in the small study next to the bedroom. It was obviously a business call, and Amanda cringed at the tone of his voice. She felt a quick rush of sympathy for the unknown recipient of his wrath. And she also felt the lingering traces of their lovemaking leave her at the same time. What was it Sam had said about him? "Inclined to be ruthless at times"? This was certainly one of those times, and Amanda resented terribly this intrusion into what should have been their time together.

She went off to the kitchen to prepare some breakfast, suddenly feeling out of sorts. But when he joined her a short time later, there was no lingering anger in his voice. He came up behind her, catching her unawares as she was about to pour some coffee, and wrapped his arms about her.

"So Sleeping Beauty has finally awakened?" He nuzzled lightly against her neck. "I thought I would have to play Prince Charming and come to wake you." Her irritability quickly dispelled, Amanda laughed and turned to receive a kiss which was warmly possessive.

He had breakfasted earlier but took a cup of coffee with her. And she could not resist commenting on the conversation she had partially overheard.

"Alex, why were you being so . . . so horrible on the phone a few minutes ago?"

He looked at her levelly over his coffee. "That was business, honey. It had nothing to do with you. I don't mix business and pleasure, and you definitely fall into the latter category." He reached across the small table to stroke her cheek lightly.

"But surely it wasn't necessary to be so brutal." She couldn't let the matter rest even though she was aware of his desire to do so.

He sighed heavily and leaned back in his chair regarding her impassively. "Amanda, I didn't reach the top by playing Mr. Nice Guy. And I wouldn't stay there long if I did it now. If you were offended at my language, I'm sorry. But I couldn't have known you would overhear it. And he has certainly heard it before."

She was not mollified. "But surely everyone is entitled to make mistakes, Alex."

He shook his head. "No, they're not. I'm not, and

neither is he. Could we end this discussion now?" Although it was phrased as a question, Amanda knew it wasn't one.

When she had finished her breakfast and cleaned up, she turned to him. "What will we do today?" She was hoping to go riding again, even though she did feel rather stiff and sore from yesterday's overexertion.

He regarded her with a lazy smile. "Actually, I thought we might just spend the day in bed. What were you thinking of?" When she blushed, he gathered her into his arms.

"I enjoy making you blush. You know that, don't you?" He began to tease her with small kisses while he cupped two big hands around her curved bottom and made her very much aware of what he had in mind. Amanda was shocked at the speed with which the fires she had believed to be banked were rekindled. And, when they returned to the bedroom, she found that they burned even hotter than before.

Much later, she asked if they could go riding. He agreed, saying that they would not go so far this time. By the time they turned the horses back toward the stables, storm clouds had begun to gather on the horizon.

"Oh, it's going to rain," she said disappointedly. The chill air already had a dampness to it.

"Not rain—snow." He smiled at her look of incredulity. "Winter comes early here and stays late. Snow in September isn't unusual here—or in June, either."

When they returned to the house, Amanda mentioned that she would like to relax in the Jacuzzi again.

"I was about to suggest it myself." He planted a quick kiss on the tip of her nose.

She undressed in her room—or rather the room that had supposedly been hers since she arrived here—and covering herself with her robe went off to the master bath.

But she stopped suddenly in the doorway when she saw him there, already in the big tub. She knew that it was past the time when she should be shy with him, but the sudden onset of their intimacies had left her slightly bewildered.

Seeing her embarrassment, he gave her a slow smile. "Surely you didn't think I was going to let you bathe alone this time? Do you have any idea how hard it was for me to stay away yesterday?" He reached out to her.

Hesitantly at first she approached him, finally reaching down with trembling fingers to undo her robe. Knowing that she was being ridiculous, she still wished that he would have averted his gaze as the robe slipped from her. But his eyes drank in her slender curves, and she almost stumbled as she got into the tub with him. He reached out to steady her and drew her to him.

Slowly Amanda got over her shyness as he lathered his hands with soap and began to wash her with sensual motions. He left no part of her untouched, and she moaned out of pure pleasure as his soap-slicked hands slid over her.

But ecstasy turned quickly to embarrassment once more when he placed the bar of soap in her hands and said, "Your turn now." Amanda's hands trembled with nervousness as she lathered them, then raised them to his neck while he held her loosely. With his encouragement, she began to relax as she moved down to his shoulders and chest. But when he pushed her hands lower, she flinched.

Alex held her hands firmly in place and encouraged her softly. "Don't stop," he said, in a voice that was, for him, very close to pleading. And she realized with a rush of warmth that she could give him as much pleasure as he was giving her. It was both a startling and pleasant discovery.

The water had grown quite cool before they left the big tub, wrapping themselves in thick towels. Before she had a chance to dry herself, he lifted her up easily and carried her back to the bedroom. After depositing her on the bed, he began to dry her, gently and thoroughly. This time she needed no encouragement to do the same for him.

They lay there for a while, just kissing and touching, and enjoying the wonders of each other. But they noticed that the room was growing cool, and Alex finally got up to light a fire and she went to retrieve her robe from the bathroom. When she returned the fire had begun to catch, and he was sprawled before it clad in his velour robe.

As she passed the glass doors to the deck, she gasped. "Alex, you were right. It *is* snowing." Large flakes were drifting slowly down from a leaden sky.

He turned briefly in her direction, giving her a wicked grin. "Mmmhmmm. We'll probably be snow-bound for at least a month."

She dropped down beside him. "You're not serious, are you?"

He circled her waist and pulled her to him. "No. Just wishful thinking."

"Only a month?" It was her turn to tease.

"Well, there is your film—and my money—to think of." He slid a hand familiarly inside her robe and caressed her soft curves.

But his lightly spoken words had disturbed her. She didn't want to think about the future.

The next morning they decided to go into town to do some grocery shopping. Amanda was dressed casually in jeans and a ribbed turtleneck sweater, with a down vest to ward off the chill. The past few days had been so filled with new experiences for her that she had quite forgotten her celebrity status.

But by the time they had crossed the parking lot and entered the small supermarket she had been made very much aware of the fact that she was no ordinary newcomer to the small town. Heads turned, conversations stopped and some mouths even dropped open in amazement as she walked very self-consciously beside Alex's tall form.

At one point she whispered to Alex that she felt guilty about being dressed so sloppily, since the public's perception of a movie star almost demanded elegance. But he laughingly insisted that seeing her dressed in ordinary clothes would only add to their memories of the occasion. "Just ordinary folk." He grinned, with a mischievous wink at her.

By the time they left the supermarket Amanda had

signed several autographs and even posed for a picture. They were both joking and in high spirits as they returned to the car with their packages. The day had grown warm, with the sun chasing away the last of the previous day's chill.

Alex made some joking remark about her star status and Amanda turned to him as they drove toward the house. "Alex, does my being a celebrity bother you?" He had been very understanding about all the attention being paid to her, but her experiences with her family were on her mind.

He gave her a sidelong glance before resuming his attention to the road. "No. It isn't my first experience with being in the company of celebrities, you know."

She immediately wished she hadn't asked as visions of Laura Shannon and Stacey Laing insinuated themselves into her mind. And once again she thought about the fact that she was no different from either of them to him. Just another one of his women. It hurt, and she turned away from him to stare unseeing out the side window.

She started nervously as he suddenly reached over to clasp her hand and squeeze it gently. "Mandy, I know what you're thinking. Forget it. You aren't like any of them."

She merely nodded, grateful for his perceptiveness. But still she wondered.

Neither of them was hungry when they returned to the house, even though it was lunchtime. Amanda had fixed a big breakfast for them before they had gone into town. Since the weather was so lovely she suggested they go riding again. But Alex countered with a suggestion that they borrow a Jeep from Dave Logan so he could show her even more of the wild, rugged country. Amanda quickly concurred and set about making a picnic lunch for them while Alex called to inquire about the use of the Jeep.

A short while later they set off from the Logan ranch in the utilitarian little vehicle. The going was easy at first as they sped along on relatively flat land. But when they began to climb into the increasingly rugged hills Amanda grew nervous.

"Will you relax? You're going to break every bone in that lovely body of yours if you continue to sit there so rigidly." Alex gave her a boyish grin as he effortlessly negotiated a particularly rough stretch of terrain.

Amanda removed her hand from the side of the open Jeep that she had been clutching for dear life. "You're going to wreck this thing, and if we're not killed, we'll have to walk back," she groused at him.

He just laughed and didn't slow down one bit. Amanda grew increasingly irritated at his cavalier behavior. The Jeep lurched and bumped along and, at one point, came frighteningly close to the edge of a precipice. By the time he came to a halt on a small plateau she was thoroughly unnerved. When he got out she just continued to sit there.

He came around and opened her door as he peered intently at her, trying to see beyond the dark glasses she wore. "You can open your eyes now, honey. We're safe—for a while anyway."

She climbed out and brushed angrily past him. "No thanks to you," she muttered.

He laughed as she turned on him. "Well, you have to admit that I got us here in one piece. And the scenery was worth it, right?"

She glared at him. "Yes, you got us here in one piece—but we still have to get back. And I didn't even see the scenery. I was too busy being scared."

"Mandy," he said in a more serious tone, "you still have a lot to learn about trust. Do you honestly think I would risk your life—not to mention my own?"

"No, I suppose not," she replied reluctantly. "But you might have shown some consideration for my fear."

He had been about to reach back into the Jeep for something, but he turned quickly at her words and walked over to her in two long strides.

She looked up at him petulantly and he reached out to brush away the fine hair that the breeze had blown across her cheek. "Haven't I shown consideration where your fears are concerned? Do you have any idea what it was like to go to sleep with you beside me and not touch you? I could have taken you even that first night, Mandy. You wanted me then and I knew it. But for some reason I can't really understand you weren't ready to accept that fact. I'm not sure you accept it even now.

"And then there's your hypersensitivity to deal with. When I made that remark earlier about this not being the first time I've been accompanied by a celebrity I could see you withdrawing again. I wasn't making any comparisons, because there are none to make. But you always seem so ready to think the worst—almost as though you wish you could find something about me to dislike."

Amanda took a few steps away from him, thinking about what he said. And she decided he was right; she *was* seeking something about him that she could dislike so that she wouldn't have to deal with her feelings. But how could she explain that to him?

Finally she said without turning, "We're not very comfortable with each other, are we?"

He came over to her and wrapped his long arms about her from behind, supporting her with his hard length as he cupped her full breasts. "No, we're not, and maybe we never will be. But some trust would go a long way, you know."

She merely nodded, relaxing against him as he lowered his head to nuzzle affectionately at her ear. She wondered if she would ever really trust him. The images of his other women returned once more to taunt her even as she responded to his touch.

He seemed to sense her confusion and withdrew from her, suggesting they climb on foot to a nearby peak, where he promised her a view worth the climb. He pulled a rifle out of the Jeep and they set off. It was rough going and though Alex, with his long legs and his strength, had little difficulty Amanda was being pushed almost beyond her limits. Once she began to slip and would have fallen down the steep incline if it hadn't been for the strong arm that reached out to grab her.

But they finally made it to the top and the view he had promised her. Seemingly endless mountains stretched out before them, jutting raggedly into a clear blue sky. The peaks were snow-covered and glistening in the sun's brilliance. Amanda breathed in deeply and held it, then finally let out her breath with a soft sigh.

She turned only when she saw Alex raise the rifle he had been carrying over his shoulder. "What are you doing?" She recalled that he had said before that he wouldn't shoot anything unless it attacked them and she looked around wildly.

"Looking for Bighorns. They frequent this area." He continued to peer through the telescopic sight on the rifle. "There's one now. Come here."

She narrowed her eyes in the direction the rifle was pointing, but could see nothing. He pulled her in front of him and held up the rifle before her.

"Hold it like this and aim it toward that ledge about two-thirds of the way up the highest peak. Then look through the sight."

She did as she was told, even though she was nervous about holding the gun. Then she saw it—a magnificent ram, standing with his head lifted. The curled horns were much larger than she would have guessed from pictures she had seen. She exclaimed happily that she had found him and continued to watch him until he suddenly bounded away with remarkable grace.

Without bothering to lower the rifle all the way she swung around enthusiastically. "He's gone. But he was so beautiful."

Alex smiled at her animation, but grabbed quickly for the rifle. "I'll have to get you some binoculars.

You aren't to be trusted with a loaded gun. Fortunately the safety was on."

Amanda's eyes widened as she stared at the rifle, now held safely in his hands. She grew really frightened as she thought of the possible consequences of her foolish action. But he saw her reaction, set down the rifle and took her in his arms.

"It's all right. No harm done. I wouldn't have given it to you without checking the safety. I'm glad you got to see a Bighorn; there aren't many left."

But Amanda was still shaken by the incident and was made even more nervous by the treacherous descent. When they reached the plateau where they had left the Jeep Alex declared that he was hungry and lifted the picnic cooler from the Jeep, while she spread a blanket on the ground.

She said little as she tried to calm herself. It had been a nerve-wracking day and they still had the return trip before them. But Alex seemed perfectly at ease as he stretched out on the blanket after they had cleared away the remains of their lunch.

He reached out lazily to her as she came back to the blanket and she dropped quickly into his arms. What began as tentative little kisses soon turned into a fiery possession, despite Amanda's protests that someone might come along. And then she quickly forgot everything in her newfound passion for him.

A day later, she was sitting before the fireplace once more; it had become her favorite place in the house. Alex was next door in his study going over some papers that had managed to find their way to his remote corner of Wyoming. Amanda was trying to focus her attention on the script for the next shooting session. Usually she was a quick study. But today she simply could not concentrate.

She threw down the script in disgust. She wanted him. She was addicted to him. It was truly frightening. They had made love so many times, and each time, true to his word, he had made it better than the last.

Finally, she could stand it no longer and decided to see if he had finished his work. She paused by the study door. He was at his desk, papers scattered about him on the desk and floor. But his head was turned away from her, toward the large window. Perhaps, she thought happily, he's having trouble concentrating too. She stepped into the room and he turned quickly at the sound. But she stopped when she saw the deep frown on his rugged face, and a momentary chill passed through her. It vanished rapidly, however, and the steely eyes became once again a warm pewter.

She went to him then, wrapped her arms about his neck, and buried her face in the springy black hair. He raised his face to hers, and she kissed his wide mouth, then the cleft in his strong chin.

He pulled her quickly onto his lap. "Are you trying to start something?" She heard the laughter in his voice.

She nodded, suppressing an embarrassed giggle. He took over then, teasing her with small kisses as he undid the buttons of her shirt. She wasn't wearing a bra. He had grabbed it from her the day before, saying that "the damned thing just gets in the way."

His hands moved restlessly over her, and she quivered with anticipated delight as he undid the top of her jeans and slid a hand beneath them. His mouth fastened itself firmly on a nipple, sucking gently. But then he raised his head for a moment and looked at her intently.

"Do you know that this is the first time you've made the initial move?" She stared back at him in surprise. It was true. She hadn't even thought about it. "I like that," he murmured as his lips trailed slowly to the other breast. "It tells me that you want me as much as I want you."

She had almost said it then—that she not only wanted him, she also loved him. But she held back, not quite knowing why. They never even made it to the bedroom, but instead made love on the thickly carpeted floor of the study, their urgency so strong that they threw off their clothes, strewing them about the room.

Her need for him knew no bounds. She writhed in ecstasy as those sure fingers found each secret place of passion and left her body aching for the satisfaction only his mastery could provide. Afterward, they sat naked on the floor and joked about the mess around them—papers and clothes scattered helter-skelter.

He told her that the papers were for an important meeting scheduled shortly after his return to work, and that he was going to find it very difficult to concentrate on the meeting when he would remember this. And, once again, she felt the future crowding in on them.

The outside world made itself known once more the next day. Amanda was busy in the kitchen preparing dinner, and Alex was assisting her when the phone rang. He answered, then handed it to her. She saw immediately a slight tightening along his jaw, and her heart lurched.

It was Sam. His call was not totally unexpected, but she had so completely put her family out of her mind that it was a shock to have them recalled in this manner. Alex discreetly left the kitchen, and Amanda found that she was being rather abrupt with her brother. She quickly felt guilty, knowing that Sam wasn't consciously prying, and stayed on the phone rather longer than necessary. She learned that he had told their parents that she was visiting a friend in California for a week, and that they had accepted the lie without question. It irritated Amanda considerably to have to lie to them. But she knew what the consequences would be if the truth were known. It was better this way. Perhaps the most upsetting thing of all was that the lie seemed to further increase the gap she was beginning to sense between her and her family.

When Alex returned, she told him that the caller had been her brother, but did not elaborate on the reason. She was grateful that he asked no questions, but she could feel his withdrawal.

That withdrawal had vanished, however, by the time they went to bed that evening. When he flung back the covers for her to join him, their bodies banished all unpleasant thoughts immediately. They lay side by side, glorying in the feel of each other. Then he slid a hand under her, to lift her on top of him. Amanda gasped as a wave of pure desire engulfed her. She eased herself down onto him and felt once again that sense of wholeness only he could bring her.

He bent his long legs and she leaned back against them, allowing him greater freedom while his hands roamed at will over her full breasts, across her stomach, and downward.

She thrust her arms out behind her, finally grasping the tightly muscled legs that supported her as he moved more rapidly beneath her. Her breath came in short gasps as the crescendo of passion enveloped her senses. She cried out in pure ecstasy. He stopped quickly.

"Am I hurting you?" His voice sounded strange to her ears.

She just shook her head, and then realizing that he might not have seen, she finally said in a quavering voice, "No. Please don't stop."

He chuckled at that and resumed the age-old rhythm until she was tossed on a wave of dazzling light, climaxing in a blue-white flame so intense that the two of them seemed welded together. Still reluctant to leave him, she leaned against him as limp as a wilted flower.

After a while he slowly lifted her off of him, dropping her softly onto the bed beside him. And he raised himself up to look down at her with a smile.

"I like it that way because I can see you. I can watch

you move that beautiful body of yours." As he spoke his gray eyes travelled slowly over the length of her.

She merely made a small sound in her throat and nestled against him.

Amanda sat once again before the flickering fire. It was their last evening together and she could not bear to think of their imminent separation. There was, finally, no doubt in her mind that she was in love with Alex. And whatever she might have once believed love to be, it had not been this bittersweet pain. She wanted to tell him how she felt, but she was afraid. It was much better to cling to the slender hope that he returned her love than to bare her soul to him only to have him thrust it aside.

He had made love to her endlessly and constantly told her how much he wanted and needed her. But he had not said he loved her. And she had seen just enough of the other side of his nature to fear telling him of her feelings.

He came into the room while she was lost in her bleak thoughts. She looked up at him as he slid down beside her. "All finished?" He had been attending to some last-minute business.

He nodded, heaving a deep sigh. "Sometimes I think that vacations just result in having to return to a worse mess than one leaves. That's probably why I take so few." He reached over and squeezed her small hand. "But this one has been worthwhile, no matter what I have to face when I return to work."

She knew he meant it and moved closer to him, curling happily against his muscular chest. She was still

dressed in jeans and a silk shirt. He had stripped off his
light sweater when he returned to the room.

After holding her for a while in comfortable silence
he laid her softly against the pillows and began to
unbutton her shirt. His hands left a tingling warmth
wherever they touched her. Then he undid the snap
on her jeans and, with one impatient motion, pulled
off jeans and panties. She lay there, assuming that he
would remove his own clothes.

But he had other ideas, and pulled her to him,
putting her hands on the belt of his slacks. Amanda
was less embarrassed about taking the initiative now,
but she was still nervous and self-conscious. She
fumbled with the buckle, finally managing to unfasten
it and slide down the zipper. Hesitantly, she tugged at
his slacks until she finally succeeded in getting them
off.

She was kneeling at his feet, and, as she straightened her back and looked at him, she was completely
unaware of what a portrait of sensual beauty she
presented at that moment—her smooth skin back-lit
by the fire, and her pale golden hair tumbling about
her delicate features.

She started to move back into his arms, but he put
out a hand to stop her. "You forgot something." His
voice was gentle but insistent.

She flushed slightly, then reached for the waistband
of his shorts and pulled them off. With a small cry, she
rushed into his arms. He cradled her lightly, kissing her
soft mouth, teasing an earlobe and softly nipping at a
satin-smooth shoulder. But after a while, he moved
her away from him, laying her down onto the deep

carpeting before the fireplace. He knelt beside her, touching her only with desire-filled eyes that travelled slowly over the curving length of her.

"Alex, please. You embarrass me looking at me like that." Her voice was a choked plea.

His only answer was a low chuckle as he bent to her. He began by touching her love-drugged mouth, then trailed slow kisses across her neck and shoulders, lingering at each swelling breast. Almost reluctantly, he went on to her stomach, then down across her thighs until he finally reached her toes.

Amanda gasped softly and held out her arms to him expectantly. Once again two bodies fused into one, heated to a white-hot fire by their need for each other.

8

Amanda strolled aimlessly through the ancient fields, a small golden figure in brown corduroy slacks and a well-worn hacking jacket. The sun was warm on her head and shoulders, but there was a crispness to the air. She came to a slow halt at the edge of the field, where a time-worn post and rail fence snaked across the rock-strewn land.

Off in the distance, her grandmother's house sat neatly amidst tall maples and oaks ablaze with the colors of autumn. It was a simple New England farmhouse, now over two hundred years old. At least the central part of the house dated back to the mid-1700s. As with so many old houses, it had grown like the proverbial Topsy, adding wings that jutted off from the original structure.

She had come here to seek the tranquility that she

147

had always associated with this place. But for the first time in her life it eluded her.

Nearly two weeks had passed since she had said good-bye to Alex in New York. For the first few days after her return to Boston, she had basked warmly in the afterglow of the halcyon days in Wyoming despite the fact that he hadn't yet called. For the next few she had told herself that he would be very busy. After all, hadn't he said so himself?

But then the day had come when she could no longer accept her own feeble excuses. Still, she had waited for a few more days before calling him, only to get his answering machine. She had wondered where he was at ten o'clock at night, as images of Laura Shannon and Stacey Laing crept stealthily into her mind. But she told herself firmly that he was probably out of town—maybe even out of the country.

Then her increasing nervousness had been finally quelled by a more powerful emotion—anger. And with that anger came shame. He had used her—and she had been a more than willing victim. He had sought diversion on his vacation, and she had certainly provided it.

But somehow, she had found herself incapable of maintaining that anger for very long. A period of intense self-examination resulted in the unwelcome knowledge that she had walked into their affair with eyes wide open. He had made no promises, no declarations of love. He had told her he wanted her, and she had discovered that she wanted him. He could not be blamed for the fact that she had fallen in love with him.

A sense of the futility of that love had swept over her like a chill winter wind off the North Atlantic, leading her to seek the solace she always found here, where the family roots went deep into the rocky soil.

There was no future for them—and never had been. Why had she been unwilling to see that before? The differences between them were too great. Had that been the reason he had shown her the squalor that had been his birthright? Was it possible that he had known even before she did that she had fallen in love with him?

Amanda was finally forced to the conclusion that a love which had grown quickly in the rarefied atmosphere of rural Wyoming would never have survived in the very real and high-powered worlds in which they both lived. She knew that others had survived such affairs without more than a temporary melancholy—but could she? It was almost time for her to go to Los Angeles to complete the film, and she missed Alex with an anguish that was very nearly physical.

Amanda stared with little interest at her reflection in the mirror. She had chosen a long gown of deep rose crepe. Tiny ruffles around the deeply plunging neckline framed the considerable expanse of shoulder and chest that lay exposed. The sleeves hugged her arms, and the slit that was almost to her thighs made her movements easier and a delight to watch. Her hair was swept up, a few tendrils curling against her face. She touched it briefly. Alex didn't like it that way. A ragged sobbing sound came from her throat.

Would she never be able to think of him without pain?

The filming had gone very well, and they expected to wrap it up just before the holidays, With that in mind, and knowing that everyone would scatter immediately after the conclusion of filming, Peter had announced a party.

As soon as the party was announced, Amanda had begun to wonder if Alex would be attending. She had been so tempted to ask Peter, but had been unable to bring herself to do so. Amanda spent a considerable amount of time with Peter and his wife, since she was staying in a little bungalow on their property. But she had carefully concealed from them the sadness and pain she felt, and she was sure that they didn't suspect anything.

Then, finally, the day before the party, Peter had casually mentioned that he had heard from Alex, who was planning to try to attend the party. Her spirits had soared to stratospheric heights at this information. But then they had plunged just as quickly as she realized that his appearance could have nothing to do with a desire to see her again. After all, he certainly knew how to find her—but had made no attempt to do so.

With a sigh she resigned herself to the fact that she had to attend the party. She had considered feigning illness but quickly gave up the idea. How could she have stood being in her little bungalow listening to the sounds of the party, knowing that he might be there? There had also been the distinct possibility that he might have wondered at her absence from the party and come to find out for himself. No, if she had to confront him, it was far better done at a large, noisy party.

As she left the little bungalow to walk the short distance to the big house she thought about the rushes of the previous day's filming. When filming had resumed after her vacation Peter had told her that one of the scenes filmed earlier in Hollywood would have to be reshot. It was a crucial love scene between Amanda and Dack. Amanda had been all too aware of her failure in that scene and had been expecting Peter's words. They had reshot it with amazing results. When Amanda saw the rushes, the memory of Alex had become almost unbearably painful. The passion she now projected so clearly had been directed at his memory, not at her costar. She wondered what Alex would think if he should see them.

The sounds of the party rushed out to greet her as she entered through the terrace at the rear of the house. Her eyes immediately sought him out. His height would have made it impossible to miss him even in this crowd. But he was not there—and her heart, which had stopped for a moment, thudded dully in her chest. Amanda was reluctantly swept up in the general merriment. All of them sensed that they had a sure hit with this film, and there was much joking about what various people would do with their Oscars.

Before long Dack found his way to her, and she was, as always, grateful for his presence. Dack was almost relentlessly cheerful and full of ironic wit, and they had become companions both on and off the set. Occasionally they attended parties together, but they spent far more time relaxing at Dack's beach house in

Malibu. Since neither of them ever read the gossip columns, they did not know that they were considered an "item" by those who feed the public's insatiable appetite for information on their favorite stars. The public didn't know that Dack had fallen deeply in love with a French woman whom he planned to marry as soon as the film was complete. Amanda did know and was happy for the man who had become such a close friend. She even took heart from the fact that Dack, who had apparently loved his late wife deeply, was able to love again. Surely that could happen to her, too.

A short while later Amanda was standing with a group of people listening to Dack's slightly embellished account of an incident on the previous day. The episode had involved Amanda, and he dropped an arm casually about her shoulders. She laughed and turned to him to protest his interpretation.

"Uh oh, I think I'm in trouble." Dack's voice was still filled with mirth, but Amanda sensed a slight tightening of the arm about her before he dropped it. She looked up at him questioningly, then followed his gaze.

Alex was coming toward them towering over the others in the room, while many stares followed him. Amanda drew in her breath sharply. Joy turned almost instantly to fear when she saw the hardness in that rugged face. What had happened to the man she had known in Wyoming? This man who now approached her was a stranger.

"Alex," was all she could say as he stopped a few feet away, while those steely eyes pierced her body, a body which still responded to him. She started to introduce him to the others, but he grabbed her hand and pulled her to him locking her in his viselike grip.

"We're leaving." The words were a taut command, and as though to underscore that fact, he quickly circled her tiny waist and propelled her toward the door. Amanda was in a daze as she was led firmly from the house. Curious stares followed them, and she was dimly aware of momentary lulls in conversation as they proceeded through the throngs.

He said nothing as he led her, his arm still gripping her waist, past the big pool and down the path to the bungalow. She had wanted him to come to her but not like this. Something was terribly wrong.

Just as they reached the little house, it dawned on her that he must have misinterpreted Dack's actions. Was it jealousy that fired his anger? She was almost hopeful. She opened her mouth to try to explain but some innate caution prompted her to close it again.

He released her as he closed the door behind them. She had just enough time to turn toward him when he grabbed her roughly and pulled her into his arms. The lips that crushed hers were merciless, and she was held in an iron grip that permitted no movement and barely any breathing. Her stunned senses tried to register that this was the man she loved, but what she felt was a stranger doing as he chose with her.

Blackness was swimming at the very edges of her vision as he picked her up and carried her into the bedroom. To her surprise he set her on her feet, rather than dropping her on the bed. Her rubbery legs threatened to give way at any moment.

The hands that pulled apart her hairdo were not gentle. But before she could protest his roughness, he was pulling off her dress, and she heard a ripping sound before he flung it away impatiently and stripped off her remaining clothes. Her trembling body registered the imprint of those rough hands and traitorously misinterpreted it.

She had not spoken, and, as he moved away from her to remove his own clothes hurriedly, she implored him silently: Please, no. Not like this. She had to say something.

"Alex, it wasn't what you thought. Dack . . ."

"Shut up, Amanda," he interrupted savagely, and she drew back from the force of his anger.

She had no time to say anything more as he pulled her down onto the bed. She struggled briefly, but he had pinned her very effectively to the mattress. She could do no more than turn her head to avoid the cruel mouth that sought hers. Even that minor victory was denied her as he twisted her chin around and reclaimed her mouth. Amanda continued to struggle with him, but her efforts had the result of alerting her jagged nerve endings to his familiar muscularity, and with a soft cry of defeat she gave up her struggles.

As he grasped her and lifted her to meet him, the cry that came from her was not one of anger or pain. It was a cry of release. And it was quickly granted as he plunged deeply into her, bringing forth the response that only he could summon from her quivering body. Mindlessly she let him lead her through a velvet mist where nothing else existed except for their joined flesh, pulsing with a life all its own.

When it was over and he still lay on top of her, supporting himself above her trembling body with arms that pressed into the mattress on either side of her, he said, in a voice that was strangely gentle, "You're mine, Amanda. You belong to me and no one else."

Hope swelled within her. "Alex, there is no one else. I love you." The words tumbled out rapidly as though she were afraid he would attempt to stop her.

Whatever response she had expected or hoped for, it was not the barely controlled icy rage on the face that was scant inches from her own. Abruptly, he levered himself from the bed and reached for his discarded clothes. She was too stunned to say anything as he dressed quickly.

Finally, as he buttoned his shirt, he turned back to her, his expression unchanged. "You're a very good actress, Amanda, not very original but very good nonetheless." He shrugged into his jacket and turned toward the door.

She pulled herself up in the bed, staring at him in astonishment. "Alex, what are you . . . ?"

He silenced her with one last ironic glance. "We've been good together, Amanda, in at least one way. Let's just leave it at that."

And he was gone.

The next day Amanda walked nervously up to the house to see Peter. She had spent a largely sleepless night trying to sort out what had happened. There had to be a reason for Alex's behavior.

She kept returning in her mind to his statement

about her being a very good actress but not very original. It was such a strange thing to say and she felt there had to be a clue there.

It suddenly came to her in the lonely hour before dawn. She had gone over and over the few words they had spoken to each other until the words ceased to have any meaning. And finally she had gotten out of bed to make herself some hot chocolate. Several pages of the script had fallen to the floor from the nightstand.

The answer had come to her as she bent to pick them up. Through her mind ran the words she had said to him: "There is no one else. I love you." Amanda felt the life flow out of her, and she sank back to the bed. Then she began to laugh and cry hysterically. What a cruel twist of fate.

In the crucial love scene she had recently reshot with Dack, she successfully convinces Dack, her much older husband, that the affair she had been having with his nephew was over. And the very words she had spoken to Alex were part of that script. Even though the mystery was now solved, there remained the decision as to what she should do about it. Her tormented mind refused to consider that, and she had drifted off into an uneasy sleep.

Now she had to find out from Peter if Alex had seen any of the film. Of course it was conceivable that he might have read the script at some point, but she considered that unlikely.

Peter and Jan were sprawled by the side of the pool and called a cheery good morning to her until they saw the dark circles under her troubled blue eyes.

They exchanged a concerned look as Peter asked her to join them.

Unable to contain herself any longer, Amanda blurted out her question. Peter looked at her carefully before answering. "Yes, he saw some of it just yesterday. What's wrong, Amanda?"

She ignored his question and asked another. "Did he see that love scene that Dack and I reshot?"

A look of dawning realization spread across Peter's face. "Yes. As a matter of fact we were discussing retakes, and as an example I showed him the original footage as well as the retake." He stopped, then added quickly, "Amanda, is there anything I can do?"

Amanda knew he had by now guessed at least part of what had happened, but she shook her head decisively, then declined their invitation to join them and walked slowly back to the bungalow.

The pieces had all fallen into place now. After seeing the great change between the two love scenes, Alex would have been forced to the conclusion that, somewhere along the line, she and Dack had become involved with each other—an impression strengthened by Dack's action at the time Alex arrived at the party.

And then she had inadvertently used the same words to him that she had spoken to Dack in the scene he had viewed—not once, but twice—shortly before. She laughed bitterly as she wondered if he knew that the line in the film had been a lie, and her affair with the nephew continued. It hardly mattered at this point.

9

Amanda found Sam waiting for her in the small sitting room of their suite at the Plaza. "Very nice. I like it." Words such as these from Sam were to be cherished, since he usually confined his comments on her attire to a raised eyebrow at a slightly daring décollettage. The subject of his compliment was a new dress of dusty blue georgette purchased that very afternoon.

Amanda was in New York for a few days to discuss a new record album, and Sam was down for the day on business. Academy Award nominations had just been announced the previous day, and Amanda was again nominated for Best Actress.

In fact, "A Texas Odyssey" was nominated for six Oscars including Best Picture, and Peter was nominated for his direction. Amanda wished that Peter and Jan could have celebrated with her, but they were in

France at the moment. She had just received a joint call from Peter and Dack, who had gotten together there to celebrate, since Dack, too, had received a nomination. Dack was still celebrating his marriage and had declared that he might just remain on a perpetual honeymoon. The call had left Amanda happier than she had been in a long while. She had eagerly accepted Sam's suggestion that they celebrate with dinner.

The glow of her high spirits was plain on her beautiful face when she entered the restaurant on Sam's arm. Recognizing her immediately, the maitre d' had been effusive in his congratulations on her nomination. Sam spoke briefly with him, while Amanda, her hand resting lightly on Sam's arm, swept the room with a disinterested gaze.

The smile froze on her face. It was Alex. He was not facing her, but there was no doubt in her mind. Few other men possessed that raven black, perpetually rumpled hair and that tremendous breadth of shoulders. The woman with him was also dark-haired and very attractive. The two of them were locked in what appeared to be a very intimate conversation.

Amanda didn't realize that she had been holding her breath until Sam circled her waist and looked questioningly down at her. She was inestimably glad when they were led upstairs to one of the smaller rooms, for she could not have survived dinner in the same room with Alex and his latest woman. The woman in question had looked directly at her, but Amanda was led away before she could see if she had told Alex of her presence.

The *mignon de boeuf en croute* was excellent, and Amanda knew that she was not doing justice to it, or to the *praline bombe*, which Sam had persuaded her to have—primarily, she decided, so he could sample two desserts. They were even visited by the French owner-chef, a tribute to Amanda's celebrity status. She told him in her flawless French that she was enjoying herself tremendously, a small lie that had nothing to do with the incomparable skills of the man. During lulls in the conversation her mind kept returning to the couple on the floor below. With all the restaurants in Manhattan why had they chosen to eat here—and on the same night as Alex?

She had believed herself to be slowly healing. There were actually days now when she did not even think about him—or at least not much. She had considered going to him and trying to explain. But the notion had been quickly discarded. He would never believe her—and what was to be gained if he did? He might have been jealous, but jealousy did not necessarily equal love. It was better left this way.

But tonight's brief glimpse of him made her painfully aware of how close to the surface her feelings for him were. And his apparent pleasure in the company of that woman demonstrated how shallow his feelings for her had been.

Somehow Amanda got through the evening, and if Sam noticed the change in her he said nothing. Amanda didn't know if Alex and the woman were still there when she and Sam left because she resolutely kept her eyes in the other direction.

Back at the hotel Sam put his arms on her slim

shoulders. "Okay, golden girl, suppose you explain to me the reason for that sterling performance tonight?" Amanda stared at Sam. So he had noticed after all. She moved away from him and sank wearily into a chair.

Sam remained standing in the middle of the room. "Mandy, you haven't been yourself for a long time. I've been telling Mother and Dad that you've just been tired from overwork. But that's not it. And I think I know the answer already. Was he there tonight?"

She threw Sam a tremulously grateful look. She was relieved to have someone to talk to about Alex. And who better than her brother, who had been her stalwart support and best friend? Still, there were some things that could not be said. So she told Sam hesitantly and incompletely about Alex. How she loved him but couldn't make him believe it, and how it really didn't make any difference since he didn't love her. And she admitted that he had been at the restaurant that night with another woman.

Sam drew a chair over next to hers and took her hands in his. "Mandy, I can't help thinking that Jay and I are to blame, at least to some extent, for this." He shook his head vigorously and continued as she was about to protest.

"We both protected you entirely too much from men. It seemed necessary for a while—after that episode at the camp—but we should have stopped. In fact, I told Jay just that. But by that time Jay was in love with you. I knew you only loved him as a brother. That's why I never encouraged it.

"But if we hadn't always been around, you might

have learned enough about men to have known to stay away from someone like Alex Wojyclas."

Sam paused and stood up, then continued. "After you announced your intention of going to Wyoming with him I did some discreet checking up on him—it confirmed what I had heard some time before." He threw her a disgusted look.

"Mandy, that man has had a string of women that would put Don Juan to shame—mostly actresses and models. Look, I'm not suggesting that he should have been leading a celibate life, but from what I heard I would have to say that he has no intention of staying with one woman."

Amanda heard everything he said, but her mind lingered on his remark that if it hadn't been for him and Jay she might have learned more about men. It was unnervingly like a statement made by Alex a long time ago. She knew now that she had paid a very high price for her naiveté.

By the time Sam reluctantly left the next morning after breakfast Amanda was feeling somewhat better. She believed Sam's judgment of Alex's character, and had almost accepted her affair with him for what it was—a difficult learning experience.

Since she was to remain in New York for another day, Sam had contacted an old friend living there and arranged for him to escort Amanda to the opera that evening. Amanda also knew Paul Scovill and looked forward to the evening. Paul's wife was in Florida at the moment attending to her sick mother, and Paul had been delighted to take Amanda to the opera for which he already had tickets.

It was Amanda's first visit to the Metropolitan Opera, and she had been duly impressed—both with the magnificent Opera House itself, with its electrifying Chagall windows, and with the dazzling performance of *Carmen*. She was unaware of the fact that she herself was a large part of the attraction that evening, as, clad in an elegantly simple black silk sheath, she was escorted to her seat.

After the performance Paul told her that he had to drop in on a retirement party in honor of a senior partner in his Wall Street firm. He asked her to accompany him and she accepted, grateful for his company.

Amanda was relaxed and comfortable at the elegant party when her composure was shattered by Alex's appearance. If she hadn't been so stunned she might have found the implausibility highly amusing. But there he was—alone this time, looking superb in formal evening clothes.

Amanda and Paul had been alone for the moment, and when she failed to respond to a question of Paul's he followed her gaze to the door, where Alex was being greeted by their host.

"Do you know Alex?" This time Paul's question got through to her.

She tore her gaze away and swallowed to rid herself of the constriction in her throat. "Yes, we've met. I'm surprised to see him here."

"CRI is one of our biggest accounts. He's quite a man. I don't know him well, but I've heard some who do talk about him." At that moment several people approached them, and Amanda seized the opportunity to turn her back to the door in the hope that he would not see her. Could they possibly leave before he discovered her?

But it was not to be. She was warned of his presence by some sixth sense a few seconds before she heard Paul speak to him. Resigning herself to the inevitable, she turned slowly to him as he shook hands with Paul. His eyes were already on her.

"I understand you two have already met," said Paul jovially.

"Yes, we have. I know every beautiful blonde in existence."" Alex inclined his dark head to her with a slight smile. Amanda successfully fought the urge to slap him. But she knew her rage was plainly evident—and worse still that he found it amusing.

As he and Paul chatted Amanda searched about desperately for an excuse to get away. Suddenly she spotted someone she had known from college—not really a friend, but she would do—and she touched Paul's arm lightly and announced that she had just spotted an old friend. She exited without another glance at Alex, but she could feel his eyes burning through her low-backed dress.

After lingering as long as she could with her college acquaintance, Amanda finally turned to find that Alex and Paul had separated. She knew that she had to get away from the party as soon as possible, and so at the first opportunity she told Paul that she had an early recording session in the morning and would take a taxi back to her hotel. Paul, of course, offered to see her home.

Amanda protested, saying that she knew Paul wanted to remain at the party. And it was at this juncture that an all too familiar voice interrupted them. That elusive sixth sense had failed her this time.

"Paul, I'll be glad to see Amanda back to her hotel. I'm leaving now anyway." Amanda knew she must have gone pale, but Paul hadn't noticed since his attention was focused on Alex who stood just behind her.

Amanda protested that she could certainly take a taxi on her own, but when Alex insisted she knew she was trapped. To continue to protest would only have put Paul into a difficult position. She knew he wanted to stay, even felt obligated to do so. She also fully recognized that CRI was a major client of Paul's firm, and Paul could ill afford to antagonize Alex. So she gave Alex a coldly polite smile and accepted his offer.

Amanda didn't say a word to him as they left the elegant Upper East Side brownstone, and Alex suggested that they walk the short distance over to Fifth Avenue where it would be easier to hail a cab. As they got into the cab, Amanda told him she was staying at the Plaza, then stared at him in shock when he gave the driver his address.

She had no desire to create a scene for the driver's benefit, since she was certain he had recognized her. But she certainly had no intention of going to Alex's apartment either. In the end she kept her silence knowing that, as soon as they arrived at his apartment building, she could insist upon his getting another cab to take her back to the Plaza. They both sat in stony silence during the relatively fast trip downtown. And as soon as Alex had paid the driver, Amanda gave him a withering look.

"Now will you please get me a taxi back to the Plaza?" Her voice was as icy as she could muster, under his dark-eyed scrutiny.

"If I had intended to take you back to your hotel, I would have done so," he said with a trace of amusement in his voice.

"Alex, I insist. I'm tired, and I have an early recording session in the morning." She wouldn't give him the satisfaction of saying that she was afraid to go up to his apartment with him.

"I wouldn't create a scene if I were you, Amanda. Doormen are well-known sources of information for the gossip columnists." He shifted his gaze to a point behind her, and Amanda turned to find the doorman opening the door to the building. The silence that surrounded them in the elevator was crackling with tension. Amanda was livid and exploded as soon as he closed the door to the apartment.

"Alex, this is unforgivable. How dare you drag me up here against my will?" She glared up at him, so angry that she had to clench her fists rigidly at her sides to prevent herself from slapping him.

He merely raised one brow as he began to tug at his tie, pulling it off quickly. "Against your will? I didn't notice any signs of a struggle."

"Damn you, Alex. You know very well that I couldn't say anything in front of Paul. He told me that CRI is a major client of his firm. And I certainly wasn't about to create tomorrow's gossip headlines by arguing in front of a cab driver or a doorman." Her voice rose with each word, and she glared at him.

"Exactly. The high price of being a star and a lady." He was decidedly nonchalant in view of her fury. There was just the faintest emphasis on the "lady."

"Lady? Alex, you wouldn't know one if you saw one. I hate you. You're a bully and a—"

She got no further. He pulled her to him, one hand catching her hair and holding it imprisoned behind her head. His gray eyes were intent upon her face. "So you hate me, do you?"

She tried to twist away from his plundering mouth, but since he held her hair, movement was too painful. Her body had already begun to react to his touch, when she kicked out at him, connecting solidly with his shin.

He growled and quickly picked her up. She hammered ineffectively at his massive shoulders and chest as he strode down the hallway toward the bedroom. "Put me down! What do you think you're doing?"

He chuckled. "What do you think I'm going to do, Amanda? I'm going to show you just how much you hate me."

Amanda didn't cease her struggles, but her anger was beginning to get all mixed up with an unwilling sense of anticipation. Being held securely in those powerful arms was an unwelcome reminder that her body belonged to him. And the certainty that he knew this angered and hurt her all the more.

He dropped her unceremoniously onto the bed, then sat down beside her. Amanda lay very still as he reached over and flicked on the soft bedside lamp. Taking her face gently in both hands, he bent over her with lips that were sensually persuasive. By the time he straightened up again, her heart was pounding so loudly that she was sure he must hear it.

When he began to remove her shoes, she found her voice. "No, Alex. Please." It was a token protest, and they both knew it.

But pausing for a moment he stared hard at her. "Perhaps you've forgotten how good it can be, Amanda?" His voice was huskily gentle. "You belong to me. You always have. Why can't you admit that?" For a long moment they stared at each other. But she wouldn't admit it, and he finally resumed his attention to her clothing.

Amanda trembled in anticipation as his wondrously rough-gentle hands touched her soft skin. When he had finally freed her of her clothing, he stood to remove his own. She watched, mesmerized, as his darkly powerful body was revealed to her. And she felt the primitive magnetic force that had bound them together since the night she had first met him.

He lay down beside her and pulled her to him, burying his mouth in the softness of her neck and hair. She longed for him—an aching, burning need that blotted out any other thought. Their bodies moved rhythmically against each other—each of them glorying in the feel of the other.

"Tell me you want me, Mandy." His voice was a deep command against her ear.

"Yes. Alex, I want you," she murmured without

hesitation. At that point she would have said anything, done anything that he might have asked of her.

He moved slightly away from her then, trailing first a hand then his lips over her yearning flesh. He was so slow when she wanted him to hurry. But nothing was neglected. He seemed determined to take his time, and no amount of urging or pleading on her part could move him. She shivered in anticipation as his lips moved steadily downward, until a firm tongue sent shock waves of desire exploding through her.

She clutched him, trying to force him to take her. And still, though she knew that his own desire had reached its peak, he took his time. When he finally pulled her on top of him, she was completely lost in an exploding passion so blinding and all-encompassing that there was no other existence for her than here with him.

She clung to him afterward as they lay side by side, arms and legs entwined. Her mind was just beginning to reassert its control over her body when the telephone rang, startling them both.

Alex cursed explosively as he glanced at the bedside phone and clock. Reluctantly, he picked it up. "Hello? Yes, Neville. Wait until I get to my study." Putting down the receiver, he looked at her regretfully. "It's an overseas call I was expecting. Sorry." He dropped a quick kiss on the tip of her nose and slipped on a robe as he left the room.

His overwhelming presence gone, Amanda began to feel a creeping sense of shame for what she had done. She had allowed him to prove once again that she was no different from his other women. Perhaps she didn't cling to him in public, but she was there at his beck and call just as they were.

She was filled with self-loathing as she scrambled from the bed and quickly gathered her scattered clothing. Having dressed quickly and given her hair a cursory brushing, she crept quietly out of the room. Fortunately, his study was located on the far side of the entrance foyer, but she could hear his voice as she paused for a second before stealing quietly out of the apartment.

She could not know how long he would be occupied on the telephone, but, since he couldn't very well follow her downstairs in a robe, she knew she had some time. As soon as she stepped into the lobby, the doorman got up hurriedly from his chair just inside the front entrance.

"Please call me a taxi," she said, trying to muster as much dignity as possible under the circumstances.

While he was outside, she kept glancing nervously over her shoulder, her eyes darting back and forth between the elevator and the front entrance. The bright yellow cab that appeared within a few minutes was the most welcome sight she had ever seen, and she almost ran through the door that was held open for her.

After giving the driver directions, she settled back with a sigh. But then, as she thought about how she must look, and the fact that she had to pass through the lobby of the hotel, she opened her small black evening bag and began to make some needed repairs to her appearance.

Her telephone was ringing when she entered her room. She had expected that, so she ignored it. After a long while it fell silent. Amanda was gambling on his being unwilling to create a scene by coming here, but she was still unable to sleep—expecting a knock at her door at any moment. When the phone rang again, she jumped involuntarily, then turned to stare at it, willing it to stop. Finally it did, and not long after she dropped off into an exhausted sleep, disturbed by dreams of what had been reality only hours before.

10

~~~oooooooooo~~~

Tension crackled through the very air of the vast Dorothy Chandler Pavillion. While others sat with a sense of nervous expectation Amanda sat numbly, barely noticing her surroundings. It had been several months now since she had felt anything.

For the past few months she had been functioning much like an automaton. "Smile a little more, please." "Let's take it again from the top of page thirty-seven." "That 'A' sounded a little flat." Whatever she was told to do she did with the determination that marks the true professional. But when she was not doing as she was told she collapsed into herself, a pale shadow of her vibrant, gracious public personality. She slept infrequently, tossing and turning with unremembered dreams. She was pushing herself hard—a new record album in precedent-shattering time, two television cameo appearances, and a popular talk show. In her rare free time she read script after script that was offered for consideration.

She was exhausting herself and she knew it. But she knew no other way to exorcise the dark torment in her life. After that night at his Manhattan apartment, Alex had made no further attempt to contact her. But she had no need to hear his deep voice or see his rugged face. He was always there in her mind.

So on this evening when she might well be savoring her greatest triumph she felt only a bone-deep desolation. "You belong to me. Why can't you admit that?" His words played endlessly in her mind—a broken record forever repeating itself. Long ago she had admitted to herself that she *did* belong to him, but he would never hear her say so. It was that thought rather than the tension of the evening that caused her hands to flutter nervously in her lap.

Beside her, Sam cast a quick sidelong glance at her. "You should be nervous. I told you to have a speech prepared." But beneath the light banter Sam's eyes were serious as he watched his sister. He couldn't help seeing the signs of nervous exhaustion, and he had astutely guessed the underlying cause.

Scattered throughout the proceedings were clips from the nominated films, and, as they were shown to home audiences, they appeared on large monitors in the auditorium. Now, following the latest round of commercials, "A Texas Odyssey" was shown. Amanda winced. She already knew that the scene being used was the beginning of the pivotal love scene between Dack and her. She tried to blot out the words that had destroyed whatever chance she might have had at happiness. And she wondered if he were watching.

Three thousand miles away in New York, he *was* watching. He had told himself he wouldn't, but in the end he did. He was already well into his third straight bourbon when the scene appeared on the screen. Pain tore through him like a bullet when he heard those words once more, but he didn't turn off the set.

His gray eyes narrowed as she appeared once more a little while later. "And the winner is . . ."—dramatic pause while the envelope was slowly torn open—"Amanda Adams for 'A Texas Odyssey.'"

The last things Amanda recalled with any clarity were the congratulatory hugs and kisses from Sam, Peter and Dack who were seated nearby. It would be months before she would see a videotape of her acceptance. As she was being escorted from the stage by the presenter, a distinguished actor nearly as tall as Alex, she looked down at the cool, smooth brass statuette she clutched in her hands. When she glanced up at the darkened wings, she began to tremble and was only vaguely aware of surprised cries as she collapsed.

She awoke groggily and looked about her without interest at first. She heard a voice, but paid it scant attention. Her senses all worked but seemed strangely disconnected from her mind.

"Alex?" The name came out as a question through parched lips. She turned slowly in the direction of the man's voice. Long seconds passed before she could grasp the fact that the face belonged to her brother Sam. And then she slipped away once more.

When she awoke again an indeterminate amount of time later, she heard again that voice—or was it different this time? She didn't think about it much but turned instead to look toward the window, where brightly striped curtains had been opened to admit the sunshine.

"What happened? Where am I?" Her mind was still working very slowly but the fuzziness had dissipated a bit.

"You collapsed, Mandy, and you're in a hospital. The doctor said it was nervous exhaustion."

She continued to gaze toward the bright sunlight as she pondered that. The Awards ceremony. She had won, hadn't she? Her mind continued to turn those thoughts over and over. But then, something else was registering. That voice. It wasn't Sam's. The prickling sensation that overtook her as she turned away from the window was strangely muted. For a moment her vision was blinded by the lingering effects of the sunlight. But then she could see the large, dark form beside the bed. It couldn't be.

"Alex?" She said his name wonderingly, still in the form of a question.

When he didn't speak immediately, she began to become convinced that she was hallucinating. "How do you feel now, Mandy?"

She concentrated on the question, not wanting to consider just how he had gotten here. "Groggy and sort of numb. Why do I feel this way?"

"They've given you tranquilizers." He dismissed

her question abruptly. "Mandy, will you come to Wyoming with me?"

Wyoming. The word reached deep into her very soul and retrieved images of sunlit days on horseback and long evenings of shared passion. He was offering her a chance to go back—back to the last true happiness she had known. She found herself nodding as she remembered.

"Good. I'll see the doctor about getting you off those damned drugs, and then I'll make the arrangements." She felt the light pressure of his lips against her forehead and then watched his tall form disappear through the door.

Time passed confusedly for Amanda. Nurses and doctors came and went. Sam reappeared. Amanda wanted to ask him how Alex had gotten there, but she was afraid he might have been only a figment of her imagination. But then he was there again—with Sam this time. And an older nurse was with them, one Amanda had not seen before. She felt slightly better, but her mind was still working very slowly.

"Do you feel up to a trip yet, Mandy?" It was Sam asking.

She nodded slightly and glanced toward Alex. "To Wyoming?" she asked in a whisper, almost afraid of the answer.

"If that's what you want." It was Sam again, and Amanda could not detect any anger in his statement.

"Yes, it's what I want." She was startled to see Alex relax immediately. She hadn't been aware of any tension in him. But surely Sam wasn't going to agree so readily to this. She looked up at him wonderingly. "Sam?" The word was full of questions.

Her brother bent to brush his lips lightly across her smooth brow. "Go with him, Mandy. It will work out."

Several days later, as the effects of the drugs wore off, Amanda was still wondering why Sam had agreed to her coming here. She had awakened that morning to find sunlight streaming through the windows of the small guest room she hadn't used on her previous visit. The first few days had been unrelievedly dark and rainy, and she had slept much of the time. When she was awake she watched television or read. She and Alex and the nurse who had accompanied her shared meals, but she saw little more of him.

On this morning, she had gotten up, showered and dressed, and left her room to hear Alex's voice floating down to her from his study, a level above the bedroom she was using. She heard just enough to know that he was on a business call.

She expected the nurse to put in an appearance as she moved about the kitchen, preparing a simple breakfast for herself. But when the woman had failed to appear by the time she had finished, she cleared away her things and returned briefly to her room for a sweater. Apparently Alex was still on the phone.

She slipped out the front door and paused to breathe in the delightful scent of pine, heightened by the dampness that still clung to everything. The air was cool, but the sun felt warm on her face as she turned it upward to the deep blue sky. Then she began to walk slowly around the house toward the back. For the first time in a long while, her mind seemed to be working properly. She hadn't taken any medication since her arrival. And the first question she asked herself was, why was she here? Coming back here could only cause more pain—and that was what had gotten her into her previous state.

Once again she wondered why Sam had acquiesced in her decision to come here. He certainly knew that she hadn't been in her right mind. And he, more than anyone else, also knew that being here with Alex was no cure.

Sam had called the day after she had arrived, but she hadn't asked him about it. The medication had still held her in its grip. And then her mother had called the previous day. Alex had taken the call while she was asleep and told her about it when she awoke. Although she couldn't detect any rancor in his tone, she guessed that he must be trying to avoid upsetting her. She had called her mother back knowing that she sounded much more like herself. But it was a difficult call, with long silences that were full of meaning—unpleasant meaning to Amanda. Still her mother had said nothing to indicate that she was displeased that Amanda had chosen to go to Wyoming rather than coming home.

Amanda contemplated this as she made her way slowly around the outside of the house to the flagstone terrace off the family room. A low wall bordered the terrace, and beyond it the land dropped sharply away in a pine-scented forest. She raised her eyes to the wooden deck perched precariously at the edge of the cliff and thought about the bedroom to which it was attached.

Surprisingly, she had thought little about Alex during the past few days. His presence in the house had caused her no discomfort. On the contrary, she now decided it seemed very right. Had the trauma of the past days somehow exorcised him from her heart? Or was she still under the influence of the tranquilizers?

She climbed up on the low stone wall and sat there placidly. But one thought kept nagging at her. Why had he come to the hospital and then brought her here? The question was still unanswered when she heard him calling her. Shading her eyes against the glare of the sun, she saw him on the deck staring down at her. And then he disappeared. A few moments later, he was striding across the terrace toward her.

A frown creased his rugged features. "Why didn't you let me know you were going outside? I've been searching the house for you."

She shrugged her shoulders apologetically. "I heard you on the phone and didn't want to interrupt you. It was such a lovely day . . ." Her voice trailed off as he stopped beside her. And then it was her turn to frown. "Where's Betty?" She was referring to the missing nurse.

"She left early this morning. She asked me to apologize for her failure to say good-bye, but there was some kind of family emergency—her son, I think." Betty had told them a little about her problem with her college-aged son.

It was then that Amanda realized why Alex's presence hadn't disturbed her. Betty's stolid presence in the house had provided some kind of buffer. But now they were alone.

"Come off that wall, Amanda, before you fall." Alex reached for her, cupping a big hand beneath her elbow.

She obligingly climbed down, her mind awhirl with the changed situation. "I'm fine, Alex. I think the effects of the drugs have finally worn off." She turned her face up to his. How could she have forgotten how very tall he was? The top of her head didn't even reach his shoulder.

He had released her arm and stood quietly looking down at her. For a moment she wondered if they could regain what they had shared here once before. But even if they could, did she really want that? She had for the most part avoided thoughts about a future that couldn't exist for them. But now she knew she could not avoid that.

She wanted to ask him why she was here, but the question wouldn't come out. And when he asked her if she would like to go riding, she nodded eagerly. And so that afternoon they went riding at the neighboring ranch, and Amanda was pleased to see the Logans once again.

Alex insisted that they not ride too far. Although Amanda had protested, in the end she was grateful for his concern. In fact, by the time they returned in the late afternoon, she was feeling very sleepy. Apologizing for her behavior, she went off to her room to nap. She had not slept well for so long, and now it seemed that she was trying to compensate for that missed sleep in a few short days.

By the time Amanda awoke the room was in darkness, and the bedside clock and her protesting stomach told her it was dinner time. She climbed quickly out of bed. Up to this time, Betty had done the cooking, except for one evening when Alex had grilled steaks. Now she assumed that the preparation of dinner had fallen to her. So she was surprised when she followed her nose to the kitchen and found a large kettle simmering on the stove. The aroma was delightfully strange, and she lifted the lid carefully.

"It's called *bigos*." His deep voice came from behind her.

"It smells delicious. Did you make it?" She turned to stare at him incredulously.

He nodded. "It's the only Polish dish I can make. It was my favorite as a kid, so I got the recipe from my sister." A short while later she discovered that *bigos* tasted just as good as it smelled. It was a mixture of sauerkraut, mushrooms, tomatoes, diced Polish sausage and apples, along with some herbs and spices.

After dinner she cleaned up the kitchen while he made several overseas calls. She thought about the fireplace in his bedroom, and wondered if he would suggest they go there. He had made no attempt even to kiss her in the time they had been here, and Amanda didn't quite know whether to be happy about that or not. But she sensed a subtle change in the atmosphere since the nurse had left—even though his outward behavior toward her hadn't changed at all.

He finally reappeared as she was finishing, and he suggested they go sit down awhile. She followed him, trying to quell a sense of disappointment. Over brandy and sherry they talked easily—much as they had done on their earlier visit here. But the big family room dispelled the intimacy that had surrounded them in the bedroom upstairs on that other trip. When Amanda finally went off to bed she found that sleep came quickly, but not before she pondered his failure to do anything more than give her a light good-night kiss on her forehead.

The next day followed the same pattern as the previous one. Amanda wandered around the house and property for a time while he spent some time on the phone. And then they went riding once more, returning late in the afternoon. As they returned to the house Amanda began to sense a mounting tension between them. This platonic relationship was a strain on both of them, she guessed. When one of them accidentally touched the other they both reacted as though suddenly shocked. Had she actually believed they might be able to be just friends?

After dinner—which she prepared this time— Amanda knew that the time had come when they had to talk about why they were here. With a mounting sense of dread, she joined him in the family room, where she found him sprawled before the fire.

For a moment, she gazed into the fire. And then she knew what it was she wanted. "Alex, would you mind if we went upstairs? I . . . I like that fireplace much better," she finished rather lamely, her face coloring as she recognized the silliness of her statement.

But he pulled himself up quickly. "So do I," was his only comment as he led her upstairs.

Amanda drew in her breath sharply as she entered

his room. She hadn't been near it since her arrival and for a moment she was tempted to flee. The force of the memories that this room held for her very nearly overwhelmed her. Only when she felt the gentle pressure of his hand at her back did she finally walk rather unsteadily over to the sunken area before the lovely stone fireplace.

Alex got the fire going quickly, then lowered his long frame down beside her a few feet away. The fire was licking greedily at the logs before Amanda could bring herself to turn toward him. And when she did it was to find his gray eyes regarding her thoughtfully.

"Why did you bring me here, Alex?" The question hung in the air, punctuated by the small noises of the fire.

"Because it seemed like the perfect place for you to rest and regain your strength."

That didn't really answer her question, and she gave him an annoyed look. But her mind had already gone ahead to the other question that had been troubling her. "I just don't understand why Sam didn't raise a fuss."

Alex laughed. "Because I convinced him that it was a good place for you, and that my intentions were wholly honorable."

Amanda was silent for a few moments, digesting that. She wondered about the conversation they must have had. Surely Sam hadn't told Alex about her feelings. A wave of panic swept over her. She risked a glance at him, and found him staring at the now blazing fire.

When he spoke, he didn't turn to face her. "Why

did you run away from me that night at my apartment, Mandy?" There was no accusation in his tone, but she thought she heard a certain sadness.

If he had been angry, Amanda might not have responded at all. But instead, she said quietly, "You forced me to go there, Alex. I just took the first opportunity to get away, that's all." How could she tell him that she had had to run from the feelings that he brought out in her?

He faced her then and fixed her with an unwavering look. "I might have forced you to go to my apartment, but I didn't force you into bed."

With an inward sigh, Amanda nodded. "No, you didn't. That's true." She plunged on determinedly. "From the moment we met there has been a strong physical attraction between us, Alex. It's taken me a long time to come to terms with it, but I think I have. I'd never felt that way before. But I've learned from it."

"What have you learned?"

She hesitated. "I . . . I guess you could say that I've learned that sometimes the body has control over the mind."

"And what has your mind been telling you?"

She looked for the sarcasm but it wasn't there. "That sometimes you can be attracted to someone you don't even like." She risked a quick glance at him, but found his expression unreadable.

"And you're telling me that I fit into that category? I couldn't blame you, but it doesn't happen to be true."

To her astonishment he reached suddenly for her and drew her unprotestingly onto his lap. "You're in love with me, Amanda. Admit it." His large hand lifted her chin until she was forced to look at him.

Quaking inside, Amanda summoned up all her acting ability and said quite firmly, "No, I'm not."

He stared at her long and hard, then finally removed his hand. His brief laugh kept her eyes on him. "Do you know, if you weren't one of the finest actresses of our time I'd believe you?"

"Alex," she said shakily, "I want you to leave me alone."

"I won't do that."

She stared at him with eyes that were misting over with tears. "Alex, when we were here before I thought you had some feelings for me. If I'm right and you feel anything at all get out of my life and stay out." She turned away in a desperate attempt to keep him from seeing her tears.

"That's precisely why I can't stay out of your life, Mandy. Because of the way I feel."

Once again he pulled her up to face him. But this time he bent to kiss away the tears that had begun to spill over onto her cheeks. "Honey, I've spent too long trying to deny those feelings. It just won't work."

His mouth tasted hers softly before he continued. "Mandy, when I first met you I wanted you as I've never wanted any woman. You're right about the physical attraction being there right from the beginning.

"But I can't truly say that I liked you. In fact there were times when I came rather close to hating you. You can't imagine what it was like to see everything I had worked so hard to acquire come so easily—so naturally—to you. All the social graces that are an unconscious part of you, I had to work at, with only limited success, I suspect.

"Anyway, by the time you came here with me my feelings had already begun to change. That's why I took you to see where I had grown up. I wanted to be sure that you saw the differences between us—in case you hadn't already seen them. I think I knew that I could hurt you, and I didn't want that. I figured that if you still wanted to have an affair with me at least you'd be walking into it with your eyes open.

"But afterward I did some hard thinking and decided that things had gone far enough. I kept telling myself that my reason for ending it was to avoid hurting you, but in reality I didn't want to be hurt myself. So I stayed away from you, with great difficulty.

"When Peter called me about the party I knew I should stay away. But I finally agreed to stop off in L.A. to see how the work on the film was going. After all, my money was invested in it.

"Peter and I had a discussion about retakes, and he showed me the original and the retake of that love scene. I think I went a little crazy, Mandy. I have a strongly possessive streak in me. What's mine is mine, and no one else's. I didn't really think there was anything between you and Dack, but I reacted to seeing you two together just the same.

"And then, when Peter mentioned that the retake had been done after the break that you had spent with me I somehow got the notion that I had been used, and I saw red. You have to understand that I'd been working too hard, and that I'd been fighting this desire to see you.

"By the time I arrived at the party something had snapped. I'll never forgive myself for the way I treated you that night, Mandy. And then you made matters worse by saying the same thing to me that you had said in the film I had just seen."

"Alex," she interrupted, "please believe me that it was purely accidental. I didn't even realize I had done it until the next morning." She looked at him imploringly.

He nodded. "I know it wasn't intentional. But I left there determined to put you out of my mind. But you refused to be put out. If that phone call hadn't interrupted us all these past months of misery might never have happened."

She stared at him. "What do you mean?"

"When you ran away that night I assumed at first that you had gotten what you wanted from me and then left. I felt used again. That isn't exclusively a female feeling, you know. I guessed that you had wanted me to make love to you but not in any permanent way.

"After I cooled down I began to suspect that you had run because you were scared. And besides, you couldn't possibly have known what was on my mind that night—I hadn't gotten to that, yet.

"By this time CRI was in the midst of a major acquisition, and I had no time for anything but work. That was finally over and done with the day before the

Academy Awards ceremonies. When I heard that you had collapsed after the award I caught the first plane to L.A.

"But Sam wasn't about to let me see you, at least not until after we'd had a long talk. I like Sam, by the way, and I think he likes me. But what was important was that he believed me enough to level with me about how you felt. And to tell me about that attack on you years ago. I wish you had trusted me enough to tell me about that, Mandy. I would have been more patient . . . at least I would have tried."

Amanda twisted around in his arms to face him. "You couldn't have been more patient, Alex. You were wonderful." Then, embarrassed by her words and consumed by curiosity, she asked, "But what did you tell Sam?"

He laughed and kissed the tip of her nose lightly. "I thought I was making that rather plain. You see, at first I assumed that Sam was just like your parents, so I told him, in my usual blunt fashion, that I didn't give a damn what he or your parents thought. I was going to marry you—and they would just have to learn to live with it." He chuckled. "I think that convinced Sam to open up and tell me everything."

Amanda touched his face wonderingly as a slow smile spread across her lovely face. "And are you going to marry me?"

"As soon as possible. Tomorrow if you like." He brushed her lips lightly with his own. "I love you, Amanda Lowell Adams Wojyclas."

And then he tipped back his head and roared with

laughter. "What a combination. The ruination of a perfect family tree."

Amanda's laughter joined his, until he silenced them both by claiming her lips once more.

When he finally dragged himself away he frowned at her. "There's just one thing more—do you suppose we could start the honeymoon tonight? I'm not sure I can wait until tomorrow."

Amanda's arms slid quickly about his neck as she gave him his answer.

Silhouette Desire
15-Day Trial Offer
A new romance series
that explores
contemporary relationships
in exciting detail

Six Silhouette Desire romances, free for 15 days!
We'll send you six new Silhouette Desire romances
to look over for 15 days, absolutely free! If you decide
not to keep the books, return them and owe nothing.

Six books a month, free home delivery. If you like
Silhouette Desire romances as much as we think you
will, keep them and return your payment with the
invoice. Then we will send you six new books every
month to preview, just as soon as they are published.
You pay only for the books you decide to keep, and
you never pay postage and handling.

Now Available

Renaissance Man by Stephanie James

Rare book dealer Alina Corey decided to live like the heroine of her favorite Renaissance book. It worked . . . until Jared Torey challenged her to leave her storybook world.

September Morning by Diana Palmer

Blake Hamilton was determined to control Kathryn but keep his heart free. She tried to rebel, until a furious Blake taught her a lesson in loving she would never forget.

On Wings Of Night by Constance Conrad

In one wild night of love Cara Williams had abandoned herself to publisher Quinn Alexander. Now faced with the prospect of working for him, could she deny the fulfillment she found in his arms?

Passionate Journey by Thea Lovan

Phillipa Bentley was swept away by passion for Raoul Mendoub, who claimed her sweetness with his plundering kisses. She tried to rebel but found this dark, enchanted prince had bewitched her soul.

Enchanted Desert by Suzanne Michelle

Jana Fleming had inherited Santa Fe's most famous gallery, but she hadn't expected artist Fletcher Logan to be part of her legacy as well!

Past Forgetting by Pamela Lind

Amanda Adams finally met her match in Alex Wojyclas, the principal backer of her latest film. In his arms she soon found herself giving in to passion's implacable demands.

YOU'LL BE SWEPT AWAY
WITH SILHOUETTE DESIRE

$1.75 each

1 ☐ CORPORATE AFFAIR
Stephanie James

2 ☐ LOVE'S SILVER WEB
Nicole Monet

3 ☐ WISE FOLLY
Rita Clay

4 ☐ KISS AND TELL
Suzanne Carey

5 ☐ WHEN LAST WE LOVED
Judith Baker

6 ☐ A FRENCHMAN'S KISS
Kathryn Mallory

7 ☐ NOT EVEN FOR LOVE
Erin St. Claire

8 ☐ MAKE NO PROMISES
Sherry Dee

9 ☐ MOMENT IN TIME
Suzanne Simms

10 ☐ WHENEVER I LOVE YOU
Alana Smith

$1.95 each

11 ☐ VELVET TOUCH
Stephanie James

12 ☐ THE COWBOY AND THE
LADY Diana Palmer

13 ☐ COME BACK, MY LOVE
Pamela Wallace

14 ☐ BLANKET OF STARS
Lorraine Valley

15 ☐ SWEET BONDAGE
Dorothy Vernon

16 ☐ DREAM COME TRUE
Ann Major

17 ☐ OF PASSION BORN
Suzanne Simms

18 ☐ SECOND HARVEST
Erin Ross

19 ☐ LOVER IN PURSUIT
Stephanie James

20 ☐ KING OF DIAMONDS
Penny Allison

21 ☐ LOVE IN THE CHINA SEA
Judith Baker

22 ☐ BITTERSWEET IN BERN
Cheryl Durant

23 ☐ CONSTANT STRANGER
Linda Sunshine

24 ☐ SHARED MOMENTS
Mary Lynn Baxter

25 ☐ RENAISSANCE MAN
Stephanie James

26 ☐ SEPTEMBER MORNING
Diana Palmer

27 ☐ ON WINGS OF NIGHT
Constance Conrad

28 ☐ PASSIONATE JOURNEY
Thea Lovan

29 ☐ ENCHANTED DESERT
Suzanne Michelle

30 ☐ PAST FORGETTING
Pamela Lind
